D1600427

Keeping You

Also From Aurora Rose Reynolds

The Until Series
Until November
Until Trevor
Until Lilly
Until Nico
Second Chance Holiday

Until Her Series
Until July
Until June
Until Ashlyn
Until Harmony
Until December
Until April
Until May
Until Willow

Until Him Series
Until Jax
Until Sage
Until Cobi
Until Talon

Shooting Stars Series
Fighting to Breathe
Wide-Open Spaces
One Last Wish

Underground Kings Series
Assumption
Obligation
Distraction
Infatuation

Ruby Falls Series
Falling Fast
One More Time

Fluke My Life Series
Running into Love
Stumbling into Love
Tossed into Love
Drawn into Love

How to Catch an Alpha Series
Catching Him
Baiting Him
Hooking Him

Adventures In Love Series
Rushed
Risky
Reckless

Stand-Alone Novels
Love at the Bluebird
The Wrong/Right Man
Alpha Law (written as C. A. Rose)
Justified (written as C. A. Rose)
Liability (written as C. A. Rose)
Finders Keepers (written as C. A. Rose)

To Have to Hold to Keep Series
Trapping Her

Keeping You

An Until Him/Her Novella

By Aurora Rose Reynolds

1001 DARK NIGHTS
PRESS

Keeping You
An Until Him/Her Novella
By Aurora Rose Reynolds

1001 Dark Nights

Copyright 2023 Aurora Rose Reynolds
ISBN: 979-8-88542-013-6

Foreword: Copyright 2014 M. J. Rose

Published by 1001 Dark Nights Press, an imprint of Evil Eye Concepts, Incorporated

Acknowledgments from the Author

Thank you so much 1001 Dark Nights for the opportunity to write for you. When I say this has been on my dream board for years that's not an exaggeration. I'm still pinching myself.

Thank you to the amazing designers and editors, and formatters who worked on this book. You are so appreciated.

Thank you to every reader, blogger, and word lover out there; I would not be living this dream without each and every one of you.

And as always thank you to my little family, my son, and husband who put up with me disappearing for hours on end to spend time with the people who live in my head.

XX

Aurora

One Thousand and One Dark Nights

Once upon a time, in the future…

*I was a student fascinated with stories and learning.
I studied philosophy, poetry, history, the occult, and
the art and science of love and magic. I had a vast
library at my father's home and collected thousands
of volumes of fantastic tales.*

*I learned all about ancient races and bygone
times. About myths and legends and dreams of all
people through the millennium. And the more I read
the stronger my imagination grew until I discovered
that I was able to travel into the stories... to actually
become part of them.*

*I wish I could say that I listened to my teacher
and respected my gift, as I ought to have. If I had, I
would not be telling you this tale now.
But I was foolhardy and confused, showing off
with bravery.*

*One afternoon, curious about the myth of the
Arabian Nights, I traveled back to ancient Persia to
see for myself if it was true that every day Shahryar
(Persian: شهریار, "king") married a new virgin, and then
sent yesterday's wife to be beheaded. It was written
and I had read that by the time he met Scheherazade,
the vizier's daughter, he'd killed one thousand
women.*

Something went wrong with my efforts. I arrived in the midst of the story and somehow exchanged places with Scheherazade – a phenomena that had never occurred before and that still to this day, I cannot explain.

Now I am trapped in that ancient past. I have taken on Scheherazade's life and the only way I can protect myself and stay alive is to do what she did to protect herself and stay alive.

Every night the King calls for me and listens as I spin tales. And when the evening ends and dawn breaks, I stop at a point that leaves him breathless and yearning for more. And so the King spares my life for one more day, so that he might hear the rest of my dark tale.

As soon as I finish a story... I begin a new one... like the one that you, dear reader, have before you now.

Chapter 1

Bridgett

Toilet Paper and Beer

Sitting in my car outside a random gas station I pulled into to fill my tank, I stare at the message I just received on my phone and feel my throat tighten—not with sadness but frustration. Two months ago today, I moved out of the house my soon-to-be ex-husband Conner and I shared. And since then, he's made it his mission to make my life hell.

Every day, it's a text or a phone call asking me to come back to him. And when I refuse, he lashes out. Why he even wants me back is anyone's guess. He doesn't love me. I mean, how could he when he's constantly sleeping with other women and has since we got married? Plus, he wants a child, and I absolutely do not.

Not with him.

I might have done some not-so-nice and really stupid things in the past, but I would never bring a helpless baby into an unstable environment. Which is the whole reason he told me he wanted a divorce to begin with. He found out that I was still taking my birth control after expressing his desire for us to have a baby. Like the decision was solely up to him.

I admit I had second thoughts the first couple of weeks after leaving him because I was really fricking scared, and my mom was adamant that I was doing the wrong thing. But now, I have zero regrets.

Actually, that's a lie. I have a whole bunch of regrets, but none of them have anything to do with moving out of the house he and I shared or contacting a divorce attorney after he didn't. Because he only used the topic of divorce as a way to try to manipulate me into giving him what he wanted.

With no choice but to text him back, I drag in a breath, then quickly type a reply, letting him know exactly what my lawyer told me just a few days ago. He cannot, in fact, take my car from me—regardless that it's in his name—so long as I pay the lease payment every month and keep the insurance up to date. Which I have.

After I send the message, I place my cell in the cupholder, then reach over and dig my wallet out of my bag on the passenger seat. With my credit card in hand, I shove my door open and place one high-heeled shoe on the ground, then the other, before hefting my butt out of the seat. Shoving my Visa into the machine a second later, I wait for it to clear. As the tank fills, I carefully watch the dollar amount since I can't put more than fifty dollars in if I plan on eating this week.

Over the last sixty days, I've learned a lot about not only who I am and who I want to be but also about money and the value of a dollar. Before I moved out of the house I shared with Conner, I never thought about how much gas was or food. Or that an afternoon at the spa costs what some people—me included now—make in a month working full time. I cringe even thinking about that.

If I had been smart, I could have been working while married instead of traveling, shopping, and pretending to be happy—*when I was not*—and saving every single dollar I made. Had I done that, I wouldn't be in the situation I am now. I would've had a nest egg and would have been able to leave Conner without worry after the second time he cheated. The first time, I took him at his word that it was a mistake and would never happen again.

All that said, I now know I will never—not *ever*—be dependent on another man in my life.

When the pump hits forty-nine dollars, I grab the handle and squeeze the grip lightly until the amount lands right on the fifty-dollar mark. As I'm replacing the nozzle in its holder on the pump, someone shouting catches my attention. I turn in the direction of the building, feeling my stomach bottom out as two men run toward me, both dressed in dark clothing with masks covering their faces. As one lifts a gun in my direction, a balding older gentleman who must be the attendant on duty yells from inside the gas station that he's calling the police.

"Where are your fucking keys?" the man closest to me barks while the one running with him opens the driver's side door to my car and gets behind the wheel.

"Got the keys!" the guy inside shouts, and my Benz's engine turns over while the man with the gun shoves me out of the way so he can open the passenger door, causing me to wobble on my heels. Then, in a blink, they speed off. I stare at the taillights of my car, sure that what just happened didn't.

"Are you okay?" I slowly turn my head at the question and come face-to-face with the attendant. "Ma'am." He grabs my arm, shaking me slightly. "Are you okay?"

"They stole my car," I whisper as my throat tightens.

"The cops are on the way." He looks around. "They emptied the register. I didn't open the safe though, so they didn't clean me out completely."

I nod. I mean, that's great, but they have my car, my purse, and my phone. And with that thought, I promptly burst into tears.

"It's okay." He pats my back awkwardly. "Come inside and wait for the police to get here." He takes my arm and leads me into the gas station that I see also has rows of snacks and other things, motioning for me to sit on a stack of milk crates near the door. I suck in a breath, trying to talk myself into calming down because things could most definitely be worse. "Here."

I lift my head as the attendant shoves a four-pack of toilet paper and a beer at me, leaving me no choice but to take both.

"Thank you." I attempt to smile, and he jerks his chin up. Looking uncomfortable, he walks off, muttering something about emotional women. I set the beer on my lap and open the toilet paper, taking out one of the rolls and using a swatch to dry the tears that roll down my cheeks.

"The police are here." The attendant stops near me as sirens rattle the glass, and red and blue lights bounce off the white walls and floor. I get off the crate and follow him outside, watching as a police cruiser parks near the entrance.

While the attendant walks around the hood of the car, I watch a familiar-looking man in uniform emerge from behind the wheel. My brother, Aiden, has been best friends with Noah since they were teenagers. The two of them played soccer and spent every minute together growing up. Even to this day, they're like brothers.

Heck, Aiden is more Noah's brother than he is mine.

My sibling only deals with me because he feels sorry for me. Well, that and because his girlfriend May is possibly the nicest human on the planet and has, for some reason, decided that she and I are friends. Even after I auctioned Aiden off at a gala we were at together—knowing she was there with him. But that's a long story I'd rather not relive anytime soon.

And Noah...well, he and I never spoke until recently. Not that we actually talk now since I can't seem to form many words when I'm in his presence.

"Babe."

Noah's deep voice snaps me out of my thoughts, and I focus on him. *How did he reach me so quickly?*

I tip my head way back to meet his gaze since the top of my head barely reaches the middle of his chest, even in my heels. Given the current circumstances, my first thought should not be how attractive I find him, but it is.

He's not classically handsome, not in the slightest. He doesn't have a thick head of hair but is bald instead—by choice, is my guess. His jaw is a little too hard, the beard covering it making it look even more so, and his eyes are far too knowing. Then, there's his size. He's at least three times bigger than most men, not just in height but also in width, and he looks like he could pick someone up and break them in half with ease.

Maybe that's why I'm so attracted to him. He's not what I'm used to.

"What are you doing here?" He drops his eyes to my hands when I don't answer, and I do the same, realizing that I'm clutching the toilet paper and beer to my chest.

"The guys stole her car, pointed a gun at her, and she's been out of it since," the attendant tells Noah before I can get my mouth to work. His eyes narrow.

"Pardon?" he asks quietly.

"Yep, pointed a gun right at her, then got in her car and took off."

"They pointed a gun at you?" Noah's gaze meets mine, and I honestly don't know what to do with the look on his face, but I can see I need to answer very carefully.

"It was for like...a second. Then they took off," I tell him quietly, and he looks me over.

"Did they hurt you?"

"No," I assure him as a muscle in his jaw twitches. The walkie on his chest comes to life, and a woman relays some information, along with an address.

"Fuck," he bites out, his jaw clenched. "I gotta go." His gaze locks with mine. "Do you have your phone?"

"It was in my car."

"I'll call your brother and tell him to come pick you up."

I shake my head, knowing I don't want that. I've already burdened

Aiden enough with my crap. He's the one I called when I left Conner. And he's been nice enough, despite our lack of relationship, to let me stay at the house he's not been living in since he moved in with May. I don't want him to have to come and get me from a gas station fifteen minutes from his house at seven at night. "I still have my credit card. I can get a cab."

Noah leans into me, and my breath catches. "I'm calling your brother. I would take you home myself, but I gotta get your car back." He starts to turn and walk away, and I panic, latching on to his arm.

"Wait, you're going after them?"

"Yeah, babe." His eyes drop to my hand on his biceps, and I quickly let him go.

"They have a gun."

"I know." He smiles, the expression beautiful but somewhat scary. "Wait inside for Aiden," he orders. Then, without another word, he turns and heads back to his cruiser and gets behind the wheel. I feel my stomach bottom out as the lights and sirens come on. I wouldn't say I've never been afraid before, but real fear courses through my veins as he drives away.

"So, I'm gonna need you to pay for the toilet paper and beer," the attendant tells me, and I slowly turn my head his way. "Unless you don't want the beer."

"I don't," I mumble. He dips his chin, then turns to head into the gas station. With no choice, I follow him inside to pay for the package of toilet paper I do not need while I wait for my brother to come and rescue me once again.

Chapter 2

Bridgett

Broke and Broken

As I'm sitting cross-legged on my couch with my laptop on a pillow next to me, I scroll through a list of vehicles available at a local dealership that offers zero down since I have no money but need a car and quickly.

Last night, Aiden came to pick me up after Noah called him, just like he said he would. And while we were in the car on the way to my place, Noah called him again to let him know my car had been totaled. The guys who robbed the gas station rolled it while being chased down a country road by the police. Thankfully, no one was hurt, including them, but they were banged up enough not to run any farther and were both arrested.

As happy as I was to find out they will be held accountable for what they did, learning that my car would not be returned to me was a blow I wasn't prepared for. With it being in Conner's name, he's the one who will receive the check from the insurance company once they finalize everything. And the chances of him giving that money to me so I can get another vehicle are about as likely as me being kidnapped by a billionaire who is madly in love with me.

Clicking on the photo of a white four-door Toyota that looks to be in good condition, I scroll through the rest of the pictures, then read over the details, honestly having no idea what any of the lingo means. If I were someone else, I'd have a friend or a friend's husband I could call to ask questions, but I don't. The friends I had with Conner have all turned their backs on me, proving what I already knew: None of them were really my friends.

Not that they would be much help since I doubt any of them or their husbands know much about cars, except what the most expensive one is and how to drive it. And I refuse to go to my parents for help. My dad has already given me a job, which is more than I deserve, and my mom's assistance would come with contingencies or a verbal lashing about how my life would be so much easier if I just went back to Conner and stopped being stubborn.

With a sigh, I get off the couch and take my cup of coffee to the kitchen. Before I can do anything about finding a car this morning, I need to finish getting ready. Then I'll walk down the street to the local drug store and beg them to use the phone so I can call a cab to take me to the police station to hopefully get my cell phone and my purse.

Halfway to my bedroom, the doorbell rings, and I turn to look at it, feeling my brows drawing together. It's early, just after six in the morning, and no one ever comes to see me. Going to the door, I lift onto my toes to look through the peephole, and my heart pounds when I find Noah on the landing. I drop to my flat feet, unlatch the locks and twist the nob, knowing it would be rude not to answer.

"Hey," I greet as I swing the door open and attempt to smile over how awkward I feel as his eyes move from the towel I wrapped my hair in when I got out of the shower to the robe I have on.

"Hey, babe." He steps toward me, leaving me no choice but to move back. The door closes behind him, something I'm grateful for since it's cold out today, even though spring is right around the corner. But having him this close, I feel like I can't even take a breath without bumping into him. He's still in uniform, including a bulletproof vest that makes him seem even larger—which you'd think would not be possible but is no less true. And he's not without his gun either. Add to that his large boots, and he just takes up so much *space*. "I thought you might want this, so I figured I'd get it to you before I headed home." I drop my gaze as he holds out his hands, noticing then he has my purse. "Your cell is in it."

I lift my eyes to his and feel my throat get tight like I might cry. And I really do *not* want to cry.

"Thank you." I take my bag from him. "I was about to go to the station to see if I could get it. You saved me a trip."

"You might want to check it to make sure everything is still inside. I don't think they had time to go through it, but you never know."

With a nod, I carry it to the kitchen and place it on the counter, opening it to find everything exactly where it was last evening. "All of it is here." I take out my phone and plug it in so it can charge, then look across the high counter that separates the kitchen from the living room. I find him still across the room by the door, but his gaze is on the couch where I left my laptop.

"You looking for a car?"

"Yes."

"Shouldn't your insurance give you a rental until you can get a new ride?"

"If I weren't going through a divorce and my ex-husband wasn't a jerk, that's how it would work." I walk out of the kitchen and go to the couch to pick up my computer and close it. "But since Conner has been threatening to take my car for weeks now, I'm sure he'll use this as the perfect excuse to do just that."

"He's been threatening you?" Noah asks quietly. When I meet his gaze, I find the same look on his face as last night when he found out someone had pointed a gun at me.

"Not like that," I assure him softly. "He's just lashing out. I don't think he would ever hurt me."

"How's he lashing out?" He leans back, crossing his arms over his broad chest.

"It's nothing." I shake my head.

"How's he lashing out at you?" he repeats a little louder while leaning into me. I flinch. "I would never put my hands on you, babe."

I lick my lips. "I know." And I *do* know that. Still, with his size compared to mine, it would only take him flicking his finger to cause damage. And even if Conner is way smaller than Noah and never hit me, he did get angry and shove me or jab his finger into my face or chest hard enough to hurt. Sometimes, he grabbed me a little too tightly, leaving bruises.

"Never." His eyes hold mine.

"Okay." I wrap my arms around my middle.

"Now, tell me how he's been lashing out at you."

"It's nothing, really. He just won't let me get my stuff and has been threatening to take the car." I shift on my feet.

"Why haven't you asked your brother to help you go get your things? Or requested a police escort to pick them up?"

"Because the stuff I have there are things he paid for, and Items I would just sell if I ever got them back. All I really want from him is his signature on the divorce papers so I can move on with my life." I wave my hand. "I'm trying not to argue with him about bags or shoes I don't actually need."

"So he's not signing the divorce papers?"

I shake my head. "Not yet. My lawyer said he has thirty days to respond. If he doesn't, we can file with the courts and wait for a date to have the divorce finalized by a judge without his signature."

"Maybe he's not happy with what you're asking for," he says. Even if he might not mean it with ill intent, it still makes me angry. I know what people think of me, what my brother thinks of me, and what I'm sure he's said to Noah about the kind of person I was. He might have been right before, but he's not anymore.

"That's funny because I'm not asking him for anything, even though I could get alimony and probably a whole lot more than that. I want nothing from him except to forget I was dumb enough to marry him in the first place."

"You married him for a reason."

"You're right. I did. Because I thought I loved him, and he loved me. Then I convinced myself that having nice things and going on trips alone made up for the fact that he was a pompous jerk and a perpetual cheat and liar." I suck in a breath through my nose, then drop my voice. "Regardless of what you might think of me, I'd rather be broke than broken." I walk around him to the door and place my hand on the handle. "I really appreciate you bringing me my bag. I know you didn't have to do that."

"Babe," he says gently, his expression going soft.

I open the door, making it clear it's time for him to go. And, honestly, he needs to leave before I start to cry. With my nose stinging and throat tightening like it is, I know that might happen at any second. "As you know, I have a lot of stuff to do today."

"Who's taking you to look for a car?" he asks, not making a move to leave like he should.

"I'm taking myself." I lift my chin while waving my hand outside, and he mutters something before walking out. I shut the door behind him, then drag in one breath and another until the urge to break down or scream at the top of my lungs no longer feels like it might consume me.

Once I know I'm good, I take my hair out of the towel and head for my bedroom, stopping when my doorbell goes off for the second time this morning. Only this time, I'm pretty sure who it is, so I don't bother checking the peephole when I reach the door. Instead, I swing it open.

"Wha—?"

"If I'm not sleeping, we're going out to breakfast," Noah cuts me off while stepping past me with a duffle bag over his shoulder. I blink at his back. "Where's the shower?"

"Umm..." I shake my head as I close the door to keep out the cold. "What?"

"I didn't shower at the station." He turns to face me. "I need to borrow yours so we can go have breakfast and then head to the dealership."

"You want to go with me?" I rub my chest, which suddenly feels funny.

"I'm not letting you go alone, babe. Those guys will eat you alive."

"I doubt that's true," I mumble, and his eyes roam over me.

"Trust me. Now, where's the shower?"

"In the hall." My nose scrunches. "Actually, in the bedroom. Aiden didn't put up a shower curtain in the hall bath, and I haven't had a chance to get one." Why am I even telling him this? "You can't go with me."

"I can't?"

"No, you just got off work, remember? I'm sure you're tired." Plus, being around him makes me nervous and itchy, like I might come out of my skin any second.

"I'll survive." He turns and starts down the hall for the bedroom. I quickly move around him to block his path. "Babe—"

"I need to do this on my own." I wring my hands as he towers over me.

"You need to get a car on your own?" He frowns.

"Yes, I need to prove to myself that I can."

"Why?" He crosses his arms over his chest.

Gah, he's relentless. "Because I've always had other people taking care of me, and I need to take care of myself for once." And that's the truth. Growing up, it was my parents paying my way. Then, when I should have been stepping out on my own, I got married to a guy who could take care of me too. I've never had to just find my way. And, honestly, it feels really fricking good when I do something I didn't think I was capable of doing.

"I'm not paying for your car, and you having someone at your back, making sure you don't get fucked over, doesn't make you weak." I blink at him because that's true, I guess. "Now, show me where the shower is."

Recognizing he won't be deterred, I sigh. "Fine." I turn for the master bedroom that hasn't changed much since my brother started letting me stay here. Really, the entire place is the same as when I moved in. The only furniture in the entire two-bedroom townhouse is the sofa, a coffee table, the TV in the living room, and the king-sized bed in the master.

As I grab a couple of towels out of the linen closet, I hear a thud. When I walk into the room, I find he's dropped his bag on the floor at the foot of the bed.

"I just need to grab my blow-drier and stuff." I hand him the towels, then scoot around him into the bathroom to get the things I'll need to finish getting ready. Once I have everything in hand, I leave him to figure out the shower on his own.

Chapter 3

Bridgett

Fancy Gadgets and Shiny Objects

With my belly full of butterflies that refuse to settle, I open the door to the hall bathroom. I heard Noah walk past the door about five minutes ago while I was doing my makeup, so I know the coast is clear.

I scoot down to my room, close the door, and then head for the closet to find something to wear. I settle on a pair of jeans and a cream sweater with ankle boots that match, then tie a scarf around my neck and grab my jacket before leaving the room. When I reach the end of the hall, I find Noah sitting on the couch, dressed casually in a pair of jeans, a hooded sweatshirt, and sneakers, with a baseball cap on his head. Where he even buys clothes to fit his large frame is a mystery to me.

"Ready?" he asks, and I realize I'm staring at him like some kind of idiot.

"Yeah, sorry. I just need to grab my phone." I quickly go to the kitchen to unplug it and turn it on. As soon as the cell comes to life, a message from my ex appears on the screen, probably from last night.

Conner: *The car belongs to me. It's in my name. I don't give a fuck what your lawyer has to say about it.*

I grit my teeth and open our chat to write him back.

Me: *YOUR car was totaled last night after I was carjacked. You can call the police station and figure out where to pick it up.*

"Everything okay?" I jump at the question and turn to face Noah, realizing that in my frustration, I forgot he was here.

"Yep, just texting Conner about the car situation since I didn't get a chance to do it last night." I tuck my phone into my bag and look up, finding Noah studying me closely. Really, the guy must be the best interrogator among the people he works with because just one look from him would have me spilling my whole life story in seconds. Like that kid in *The Goonies* who told the puking story when he was picked up by the bad guys after his friends. "I'm ready if you are."

He steps to the side, and I walk to the door as he grabs his bag from the floor next to the couch. When we get outside, I lock up. But instead of heading for the parking lot, he stands behind me like some kind of oversized sentinel, making me feel awkward. When I'm done, we walk down the sidewalk. Having seen his truck before I'm not surprised by its size. If he were a different man, I would assume he was attempting to make up for some physical attributes he lacks, but the lifted black-on-black 4x4 fits him perfectly. And, really, he would look odd getting into a smaller vehicle.

Instead of going right to the driver's side, he walks me to the passenger door and opens it for me to get in. It takes a couple of tries to get my ass up into the seat, but when I finally do, he closes the door before heading around the truck bed. As I put on my seat belt, I look around the interior. There's not an upgrade in sight, and something about that causes me to relax. He's a normal guy—just a nice, normal guy—not one impressed by fancy gadgets and shiny objects.

"Where do you want to eat?" I ask as soon as he opens the door, before he even has a chance to get behind the wheel.

"Have you been to Maple Biscuits?" he asks, and I shake my head. He flashes a grin that causes those pesky butterflies to speed up. "You're in for a treat."

He starts the engine and backs out of the parking spot before putting on his seat belt. As he drives, I pull up the menu for the restaurant on my phone, wanting to make sure I have enough money to cover his meal and mine, then inwardly groan when **Conner Calling** appears on the screen.

"You gonna answer that?" he questions, and I want to say no, but given what happened last night, I know I don't have a choice.

"Unfortunately," I mumble, then click the green phone symbol and put it to my ear. "Conner."

"You were carjacked?" he shouts in greeting, and I pull the phone slightly away before answering.

"Yes."

"This wouldn't have happened if you'd just fucking come home already, Bridgett."

"It could have happened anywhere. And, as I told you before, I'm not going back."

"What do you want from me?" he yells. I can picture his handsome face—red with anger—and his hair a mess because he always rips his fingers through it when he's mad or not getting his way. "Do you want me to write my name in blood and say I'll never cheat again? That I'm okay with not having a kid? If that's what you want, I'll do it."

"All I want is for you to sign the divorce papers." I keep my tone even, knowing he's already on edge.

"Fuck you! You think I can't have better than you? That I can't *do* better than you?" he rages in my ear. "You're the worst lay I've ever had, and you wonder why I cheated every fucking chance I go—"

His words end when Noah snatches the phone out of my hand. I jerk my head to the side to watch in horror as he puts my cell to his ear and growls, "Do not call her number again. If you need to get information to her, have your lawyer talk to hers." And with that, he disconnects and dumps my phone in the cupholder between us, then turns to look at me. "You are not talking to him."

"You just—"

"Never again, Bridgett," he cuts me off. "That guy..." His jaw clenches. "Never again."

With my throat tight and my face feeling like it's on fire, I nod. Obviously, he heard what Conner said. If that isn't humiliating, I don't know what is. It's not the first time Conner has blamed his infidelity on me, but knowing that someone else heard him? That *Noah* heard him say I'm so bad in bed he had to go elsewhere, it's...well, I don't even know what it is.

I stare out the window for the rest of the drive, refusing to give in to the urge to cry like I want to. Unluckily for me, we reach the small plaza where the restaurant is, and far too quickly. With my insides twisted into a knot, Noah parks his truck. As soon as he comes to a stop, I hop out, needing a second of fresh air to pull myself together a little more. Especially before I have to sit across from him in a restaurant with no choice but to face him.

"Yo!" he bites out. I spin around and find him storming in my direction. "Next time you get out of my truck before I've even put it in park, we're gonna have a problem."

"Wh...? What?" I back up a step as he closes in on me.

"I get you're upset about what that douchebag you married said, but you will not put yourself in danger. Do you understand?"

"I wasn't in danger," I say quietly. He makes a deep growling sound in the back of his throat that causes the hairs on the back of my neck to stand on end as his eyes narrow scarily. "I mean, okay," I quickly amend.

"Okay," he grumbles, not looking any less angry. I shift on my feet as his eyes bore into mine.

"Should we go eat?" I blurt, wanting to end the awkward stare-down between us.

"Yes." He grabs my wrist, startling me. My skin burns from his touch—not in a bad way, but in a way that makes me very aware of his proximity—and I oddly miss it when we reach the restaurant, and he lets me go to open the door.

When we get inside, I see people standing near the entrance, waiting to be seated, and the entire dining area is packed. We get in line, and I look around, noticing that many of the patrons have their eyes on Noah. Not just women but also men. I wonder if he always draws so much attention everywhere he goes.

"Is it just you two?" A young woman who's probably still in high school greets us with a smile when we finally reach the podium.

"Yep," he tells her, and she drops her gaze to the paper in front of her, then looks between Noah and me.

"It's going to be about ten minutes. Is that okay?"

"That works for us." He lifts his chin, then gives her his name. She writes it down on the list.

As we move to stand in the alcove near the front door with everyone else, a handsome man with gorgeous dark skin, dressed in jeans and a thermal shirt with a vest over it, approaches us with a blinding-white smile. There's a woman on his arm that I swear must be a model. If she's not, she should be. Like the man's, her skin is flawless, and her tall, thin frame would make most designers cry with happiness. I mean, honestly, even in the jeans she has on with a turtleneck and trench coat that matches her pointy boots, she looks like she should be on a runway.

"Noah." The man gives Noah a fist bump. "I was just talking about you this morning."

"Oh, yeah?" Noah asks while the woman leans in to give Noah a one-armed hug with a smile to match her guy's. I stand slightly away, feeling awkward and out of place.

"Heard you tossed your hat into the ring for detective."

"I did," Noah tells him, and I tip my head back to look at him, in awe of the news because I'm sure it's a big deal.

"If they don't give it to you, I've got a desk in Nashville with your name on it."

"I appreciate that, man," Noah says quietly.

"Just speaking the truth. They'd be stupid not to give you what you want, especially when you've been helping them solve cases without the title," he says, and Noah places his hand against my lower back, sliding it around my waist to pull me closer to his side.

"Babe, this is Sergeant Devon Marshall and his wife, Nova. This is my best friend's sister, Bridgett."

"Nice to meet you both." I fiddle with the handle of my bag in front of me as Nova looks between Noah and me.

"Your best friend's sister?" Nova raises a brow, her eyes landing on Noah. "That sounds complicated."

"We're just friends," he tells her, and I chew the inside of my cheek. *That's a stretch*, I think. We've only been around each other a handful of times over the last couple of months and have barely spoken.

"Hmm." She meets my gaze. "I love your scarf and bag."

"Thank you." I touch the Burberry scarf around my neck, one I have plans to sell and probably shouldn't be wearing. "I love your whole outfit."

"Thanks." She smiles at me, then leans into her husband. "We should go before your mother kidnaps our children."

"I wish she would," Devon tells her, and she smacks his chest, making him laugh. "All right, all right. It was nice meeting you, Bridgett. And, Noah, I expect a phone call if things don't work out."

"You'll hear from me," he replies. Nova gives us a wave while Devon lifts his chin. When they leave, I look up at Noah and start to open my mouth to ask about him wanting to be a detective, but a woman approaches carrying two menus.

"If you'll follow me." She smiles, then turns. We walk behind her, wending through tables to the back of the room and a corner booth just big enough for two.

I remove my jacket and start to take the seat facing the restaurant but stop when Noah carefully moves me to the bench on the opposite side of the table. He waits until I'm seated before sliding into the booth across from me.

Well, okay then.

"I'm Holly and will be your waitress this morning. Would either of you like coffee or a mimosa while you look this over?" She hands each of us a menu.

"I would love a cup of coffee, please." I smile at her. She smiles back, then looks at Noah, who asks for the same.

"I'll be right back." She takes off, and I tuck my bag and coat into the space next to me, lifting my eyes to Noah and finding him scanning the room.

"So, you want to be a detective?"

At my question, his gaze moves to me, and he relaxes in his seat. "Yeah." He takes off his hat. "I've been working toward it for a while now, but my station is small, so there's not much turnaround."

"But something opened up?" I guess, and he nods.

"A week ago, a detective retired, and a spot became available. A few of us applied for the position, so now we have to wait and see who gets chosen."

"You'll get it," I tell him, then lean back when Holly stops at the end of the table to drop off our coffees.

"Do you two need a few more minutes?" she asks.

"Yes, please," I tell her. She nods before taking off once more. With her gone, I take the tiny pot of creamer she set down, dump some into my cup, then pass it to Noah. "And it sounded like if you don't get it, you can get that position somewhere else."

"Except I don't want to go anywhere else," he tells me while pushing a container of sugar packets toward me.

"Why not?"

"I love my town, the people here, and the men and women I work with. Not saying there's anything wrong with Nashville, but I've never had a desire to work in the city."

"I can understand that."

"Do you miss living near the city?" he asks, and my nose scrunches.

"No. I mean, I miss Starbucks being just a two-minute drive from my house and not having to go so far to get to the grocery store, but I don't miss the city and its traffic." I pick up my coffee and take a sip, then grab the menu from where I placed it and start looking it over, figuring I should find something to eat before Holly comes back. "So, what's good here?"

"Everything," he says, and I smile at him.

"That's not helpful."

"But it's true," he replies. I settle on a biscuit breakfast sandwich with ham, egg, and cheese.

And he's not wrong. It's delicious. But what is even better is enjoying it while sitting across from him. Because even if the morning started off strange, by the end of breakfast, my nerves have settled, and all the awkwardness from earlier is long gone.

Chapter 4

Noah

Ignore It

Sitting next to Bridgett in a chair three sizes too small in an office at the car dealership, I listen to Hunter, the loan specialist, explain the limited warranty the car comes with. As he carries on, I glance over at Bridgett and find her looking adorably confused and cute as fuck as she jots down notes on a notepad while nibbling on her bottom lip. When I started thinking of her as *adorable* and *cute* is something I can't figure out, especially when I just thought of her as Aiden's stuck-up, bitchy little sister for years.

What I do know is that I need to shake off the urge I have to protect her. Particularly when that urge comes from a place that has nothing to do with her being my best friend's little sister and everything to do with the fact that she is a beautiful fucking woman who is going through some fucked-up shit.

"What do you think?"

Her question drags me out of my thoughts, and I dip my chin to meet her gaze.

"About what?" I ask as Hunter leaves the small office we have been in for the last forty-five minutes.

"About the car."

"I already told you, babe. It's a nice vehicle, and the price is right," I say, and she chews on her bottom lip, a tic of hers that causes me to shift on the small-ass chair.

"You did say that."

"What has you second-guessing your decision?"

"I don't know. I guess that it's *mine*, and I don't want to get something only to turn around and wish I hadn't."

"You have ten days to change your mind after you pull off the lot."

"I guess you're right." She lets out a breath, then drops her gaze to the notepad on her lap. "And the car payment including insurance is less than what I pay now, so that will be a big relief each month."

"You're working for your dad now, right?"

"Yeah." She ducks her head, and color spreads up her cheeks.

"There's nothing wrong with working for your dad."

"I know. It's just...getting coffee, answering phones, and running errands isn't something I want to do forever." She lifts one shoulder. "Especially when I know that isn't a position that actually existed before I went to my dad to ask for a job."

Hearing the sadness—or maybe it's dejection—in her voice, I have the urge to pull her onto my lap and just hold her. It's the same feeling I had this morning when she laid shit out about why she'd been with her ex and why it hadn't worked out between them. Then again, after hearing that douche spew bullshit at her, it's no wonder she didn't want to stick around, even with vacations, a fancy house, and expensive clothes.

Being friends with Aiden since we were kids, I learned firsthand how tumultuous his relationship with his family was. His parents were selfish and

self-righteous—his mother still is. His father, who recently suffered a stroke, has gotten better, but who knows if that will last. And Bridgett, she was the little sister he didn't pay much mind to. When they got older, he would just talk about how spoiled she was and how much she reminded him of his mom.

But after hearing what she said this morning and right now, I wonder if, like her brother, she was looking for a way out. Only instead of going away to college and then eventually playing soccer in London like Aiden, she got married, hoping to escape. Obviously, that didn't work out. Now, she's pushing herself to do the complete opposite of what she did before.

"All right, the guys are putting the temporary plate on your car as we speak," Hunter says as he walks back into the office. "As soon as they're done, they'll pull it around front." He holds out a single key. "This is your spare. If you have any issues, just give us a call."

"That's it?" she asks as she takes the key from his grasp and clutches it in her fist.

"That's it. Your paperwork is all signed. You're free to go."

"That was easier than I thought it would be."

"Glad to hear it." He chuckles as we both stand. "Nice meeting you both." He lifts his head to look me in the eye. "I saw your truck out front. If you're ever in the market for an upgrade, come back here. We'll hook you up."

"I'm good, but thanks." I reach out my fist, and he bumps it before I place my hand against Bridgett's lower back to steer her out of the office.

When we get outside, her new-to-her Toyota is parked next to the curb with the engine running, so I walk her around to the driver's side door and open it. As she stops, she tips her head back and locks her eyes with mine.

"Thank you for coming with me today. I would have been lost without you."

"No, you wouldn't have been," I tell her quietly because I know she needs to hear that she's capable of doing these things on her own.

"Still, I appreciate it a lot." Her fingers play with the handle of her bag. One that probably costs more than I make in a month. "Do you work tonight?"

"I've got the night off." I watch her nod. As she licks her lips, my attention instinctively drops to her mouth. Shit, I need to get out of here. "All right, babe, drive safe." I take a step back.

"I will." She lets out a breath. Then, in the blink of an eye, her tits are pressed against my abs, and her arms are around my back. I return her hug on instinct and tell myself to ignore the fact that she feels good in my arms. That her soft curves feel perfect pressed against me. "Thanks, Noah." She lets me go, and I let my arms fall to my sides.

"Anytime, babe." I watch her get into her car. Once she's seated, I shut the door. She smiles up at me through her closed window, and my chest feels strange. But I tell myself to ignore that shit too as I take a step back and watch her drive off.

With a shake of my head, I walk across the lot to my truck and get behind the wheel to head home.

Where I do not get any fucking sleep.

Chapter 5

Bridgett

Mommy Dearest

Looking through the possible answers on the online practice realtor exam, anxiousness begins filling the pit of my stomach. I've been studying every night after work for the last two weeks, and I still feel like I know little to nothing at all. After clicking on one of the multiple-choice answers, I let out a sigh of relief when a plethora of fireworks fill the screen, signaling that the test is over, and I passed.

"When is your test?" I spin in my chair at the question and find Edgar, one of the older gentlemen who has worked for my dad forever, standing behind me with a sour expression on his weathered face. Like most people who work in the office, he's made it very clear that my presence is unwanted and unneeded and that the only reason they tolerate me is because my dad owns the company.

"In two weeks." I rub my palms down the front of my slacks before standing and pushing in my chair.

"Do you think you should be practicing while you're here at work?" he asks, and even though his tone is even and nonconfrontational, I can tell by his expression it's anything but.

"I'm actually on lunch right now." I grab my purse from the small cabinet behind my desk. "I was just taking a few minutes to practice the test before I went out to find something to eat." I give him my sweetest smile. "Do you want anything from the coffee shop?"

"Not right now." He tucks his hands into the front pockets of his slacks and, without another word, walks away, heading toward the offices that line the hall. I'm sure he'll complain about me to anyone who will listen. I can't even count the number of times I've overheard him and everyone else who works here talking about me behind my back. It sucks and makes it difficult to show up every day. But I need this job, at least until I get my license and can start working somewhere else.

As I'm heading toward the front door to leave, I spot my mom through the glass as she walks toward the building. My first instinct is to turn around and run in the opposite direction to find somewhere to hide until she passes, but as her gaze locks on mine, I know it's too late.

Great, just what I need today.

"Mom," I greet as I shove the metal-framed door open, not even a little shocked that she doesn't smile or even attempt to give me a hug when she's standing before me. My mother has never been the kind of mom to show physical affection, unless it's a kiss on the cheek at a public event, but that's just for show.

"I was coming to see you. Are you leaving for the day?"

"No, I was heading out to get something to eat from the coffee shop down the street." I motion to Steam, which is just a couple of doors down from my dad's office.

"I'll join you."

Great. I inwardly groan. This just keeps getting better.

"Is everything okay?" I ask as she falls into step with me.

"Your dad asked me for a divorce," she says, like she's letting me know what color the sky is. I stop in my tracks.

"What?" I turn to face her, sure I misunderstood.

My parents have been together since my mom was twenty-three and my dad was twenty-six. I wouldn't say it was an arranged marriage, but it still kind of was. My mom's mother searched until she found someone suitable for her daughter to marry, and that someone happened to be my dad. And Dad's parents both insisted that my mom would be a good pick for him and pushed him to propose. It wasn't a love match, nor was it a situation where they learned to love each other over time.

They both resented each other, which led to each of them being vindictive. They should never have wed and really shouldn't have stayed married. Still, I assumed they would live out the rest of their days together, even if they were miserable doing so.

"It seems your father has decided he no longer wishes to be married to me." She lifts a delicate hand between us. "As you know, he's been different since his stroke. So he may change his mind and not go through with this ridiculousness."

"I... Wow, okay." I shake my head, trying to get my thoughts in order because this is a lot to take in. I mean, my dad *has* seemed different since his stroke a few months ago. But if I almost died, then became paralyzed on one side of my body and had to go through intensive therapy, I would probably start looking at life a little differently as well. "What are you going to do?"

"I'm going to talk to a lawyer and find out what I'm entitled to." Her eyes wander over my face. "As you should be doing for yourself."

My stomach twists. "I don't want anything from Conner."

"You really must stop being so immature, Bridgett. You were married without a prenup and deserve at least half of what he has."

"I didn't go to work with Conner every day, so I don't deserve anything from him except his signature on our divorce papers. And that is honestly all I want."

I look into eyes the same color and shape as mine. I let her manipulate me for years and went along with whatever she said out of some stupid need to earn her love and gain her approval—which was a waste of effort on my part. I don't think she knows what love is, and I doubt she is capable of loving anyone but herself.

"You're making a mistake. You should at least talk to Conner and try to work things out with him."

"He cheated on me and treated me like garbage. I know I've said it before, but hopefully you'll hear me this time." I grit my teeth as I try to get control of the temper I feel slipping. "I'm never getting back with him. I have no desire to live my life never feeling real happiness. Never finding someone who loves me just for me. Having money might be nice, but being able to look at myself in the mirror every day without hating the person looking back at me feels really flipping good. And I would rather be alone than lonely, which is what I was when I was married."

I take a step away from her. "I'm going to get a coffee before I have to go back to work. I'll talk to you later." I walk away without looking back and head down the block to the coffee shop. I'm thankful she doesn't follow.

After placing an order for a large coffee and a turkey sandwich on rye, I sit at one of the tables and grab my cell phone out of my purse. Staring at the dark screen, I try to think of someone I can call or message just to get the confrontation out of my head, but there's no one. I don't have any friends anymore, and I can't even message my brother to tell him that our parents are getting divorced or to bitch about our mom.

It wasn't a lie when I said I would rather be alone than lonely. But maybe it's because I have always been lonely and am used to it now.

Chapter 6

Bridgett

Drinks

Standing in my kitchen, I look down at the cookies I just pulled out of the oven. I don't know where I went wrong, but it's obvious I made a mistake somewhere because my cookies do not look anything like they're supposed to. In fact, they look more like overcooked pancakes with chocolate chips than anything else.

Ken, who was my family's chef growing up and still cooks for my parents, would be highly disappointed if he saw this disaster. When I was little, I would sneak into the kitchen to hang with him whenever I knew my mom wouldn't be around. Because Lord knows she would have lost her mind if I told her I wanted to learn to cook and actually enjoyed it. But Ken let me help him anytime I asked and showed me all his tips and tricks for making everything from breakfast to fancy desserts. Obviously, I've lost my touch over the last few years.

I shake my head with a groan. Maybe trying to bake Noah cookies was a stupid idea. I don't even know if he eats sweets. With a body like his, I doubt he does. Using the spatula, I scrape one of the cookies off the tray and take a bite, shrugging at my discovery. They might look like garbage, but they actually taste delicious.

I hear a knock on the door and frown. Heading out of the kitchen toward it, I check the peephole to see who it is—all while praying it's not my mother. After the confrontation we had earlier today, I'd be happy not seeing her for a very, very long time. But with plans to visit my dad tomorrow after work, I doubt I'll be that lucky. Because even if my father asked her for a divorce, I'm sure she will still be at the house, making her presence known.

A smile curves my lips, and I swing open the door when I see my brother's girlfriend, May, on the porch.

"Hey, what are you doing here?" I ask as she steps inside to greet me with a tight hug. The first time she ever hugged me, it completely caught me off guard, and I honestly didn't know what to do. My family did not hug growing up, and no one else I know is big on hugs either. But…it's nice.

"I was driving by and thought I'd stop in to see if you'd be interested in going out with me for a drink."

"Right now?"

"Yes." She laughs. "I know you've been working a lot lately, and we haven't had a chance to catch up."

"I'd love to go." I watch her smile before she looks around with her nose in the air.

"What smells so good?"

"I was making cookies for Noah and—"

"You're making cookies for Noah?" she cuts me off, her eyes wide.

"Yeah." I head back to the kitchen. "The day after my car was totaled, he stopped by to bring me my purse and saw that I was looking for a new vehicle." I lift one shoulder. "He took pity on me and drove me to the dealership, so I wanted to thank him. And since I don't have a lot of money, making something homemade seemed like the best idea."

"I didn't know your car was totaled." She rests the palm of her hand against her chest. "Aiden didn't tell me that."

"It's not a big deal." Really, I'm not surprised my brother didn't tell her. I know he wants to protect her, and that includes safeguarding her from me. I grab one of the fast-food containers I washed and saved to use as Tupperware later and start loading the cookie dough into it.

"It *is* a big deal. He should have told me." She shakes her head and lets out a breath.

"Don't be mad at him. I'm sure he just didn't think about it. And it's okay. Noah helped, which was really kind."

"And now you're making him cookies."

"I was, but this batch was no good. I'll have to redo them," I say. She picks one up off the pan and takes a bite.

"They're delicious. What recipe did you use?"

"I didn't use a recipe."

"You didn't?" Her brows dart together.

"No, I have it memorized since it's one Ken and I used to make all the time when I was little."

"Ken. Your parents' chef, Ken?" she asks, and I know Aiden must have mentioned him to her at some point.

"Yep."

"You used to bake with him?" she asks, sounding surprised.

"Yeah, I was always in the kitchen annoying him when I was little. Really, I bothered him even when I was in high school."

"Did your brother ever hang with him?"

"No, he was always gone with Noah and wasn't really around very much," I say. She looks thoughtful as she studies me closely. Needing to get out from under her scrutiny, I take the dough to the fridge and set it inside, asking, "Do you think I need to change?" I glance down at the jeans and sweater I put on when I got home from work this evening.

"I'm wearing what I wore to work today, so you're good."

"Cool." I place a layer of foil over the cookies that are already done and then grab my bag off the counter.

"Do you want me to drive?" I pick up my jacket from where it's lying on the edge of the couch and put it on.

"I can drive us." She opens the door, and I follow her out of the house and stop to lock up. "Which one is your new car?" she asks, and I turn around to face the parking lot.

"The white Toyota."

"Nice." She walks over to check it out. "Do you love it?"

"Yes." I feel oddly proud of my new car. It's not the nicest one I've ever owned, but it's mine. I paid for it—or *am* paying for it—all by myself, which is huge.

"I'm glad you found something." She clicks the alarm for her vehicle, and I get in on the passenger side while she gets behind the wheel.

The drive to the wine bar takes less than twenty minutes, and when we get inside, I'm surprised by how modern and hip the space is. The backlit bar, dim lighting, concrete floors, and well-spaced tables make it feel like a place you'd find in a big city somewhere.

"Hey." A handsome guy with the whole hipster thing going on greets us at the door. "Are you two looking for a table or wanting to sit at the bar?"

"I think a table." May looks over at me, and I nod.

"Cool, follow me." He heads toward the back of the room and shows us to a small table with two chairs. "You can pull up the drink menu using the QR code on this." He points to a stand in the middle of the table. "Or you can get a wine card from me and use it at that wall there." He points to a wall lined with fancy machines and wine bottles behind glass. "I'll give you a couple of minutes to decide."

"Thanks," May and I reply at the same time, and he smiles at the two of us before taking off.

"Are you having wine?" I grab my phone so I can scan the code.

"I don't know. I'm not really in the mood for wine." She scans the code herself. "Oh, they have a raspberry martini."

"That sounds good." I look over what they have to eat since I'm actually starving. "Do you want to share a cheese board with me?"

"Yes, I'm so hungry. I didn't really have a chance to eat lunch today."

"Is everything okay?" I focus on her, feeling concerned. A few weeks ago, a senior in her school tried to shoot Aiden and actually ended up hitting another teacher. Apparently, the kid was secretly in love with her and wanted my brother out of the way. I had no idea until I heard about the shooting on the news.

Not that I was surprised my brother never mentioned anything. He might be letting me stay at his place, but our relationship hasn't changed at all.

"Oh, yeah, we have the school book fair this week, so it's been really busy."

"I used to love going to the book fair. I didn't know that was still a thing."

"It is, and the high school hosts it twice a year for the smaller schools. It's a lot of fun."

"I bet." I smile, then look up at our waiter when he stops next to our table.

"Are you ladies ready to order?"

"I think so." I look at May.

"Yep." She rattles off the drink she wants, and I go with a Moscow mule and order the cheese board for us to share. "So, how has work been?" she asks when the waiter walks away.

"Okay, but I can't wait to get my license and find something else."

"You don't like working at the office?" She tips her head to the side as she studies me.

"Everyone there has made it very clear I'm not wanted." I let out a dry laugh, and her expression softens.

"I'm sorry."

"It's fine. I mean, I knew going in that the only reason I got the job is because my dad owns the company."

"I guess." She scrunches her nose. "So how are things moving along with Conner and *that* whole situation?"

"He still hasn't signed the papers, but my lawyer assured me that he can't prevent the divorce from going through in the end. That made me feel better about the whole thing."

"Has he said why he's not just signing them?"

"No." I look across the room when I feel like someone is watching me and find a group of women gathered at the bar—all of whom I used to talk to regularly. None of which I talk to anymore since they are all married to or dating Conner's friends.

"Do you know them?" May whispers, and I focus on her.

"Yeah," I whisper back, then jump slightly when our waiter places two glasses on the table in front of us. "Thank you." I tip my head back to look up at him and catch his smile.

"Your board will be out in just a couple of minutes, but if you need anything between then and now, just let me know."

"We will." May picks up her glass and holds it out toward me as he walks off. "Let's toast." I pick up my glass and hold it close to hers.

"What are we toasting to?"

"To drinks with friends." She smiles, and I feel my muscles relax. I know my brother would likely prefer that his girlfriend and I were not friends, but I honestly couldn't be more thankful for May's constant support and acceptance. Especially now when I feel so alone.

"I'll drink to that." I tap my glass against hers, then take a sip, hoping to calm my nerves that seemed to come to life after seeing who was at the bar.

"Bridgett?" My spine stiffens at the sound of my name in a very familiar voice. I swing around and watch Molly approach with Vanessa and Catharine. "I thought that was you." She gives me a sugary-sweet smile before leaning down to press the side of her lips to my cheek. "How have you been?"

"Good." I touch my fingers to my face, sure she left behind some of the bright red lipstick she has on. "How are you?"

"Fabulous." She smooths her hand over her hip, drawing attention to her small waist and the large, sparkling diamond on her finger. "Busy, actually. Brayden and I are working on having a baby."

"Good for you." I keep my face neutral, knowing for a fact that her marriage is just as preposterous as mine was. She and her husband have been together for three years and married for one. In that time, I know he's cheated multiple times, and so has she. I can only imagine that all their dysfunction will lead to disaster sooner or later, which will suck for any child they have together.

"I heard you've been working for your father."

"I have." I keep my answer short, hoping she'll get that I have no desire to pretend we're friends or think that she actually cares about what I've been doing.

"Are you going to continue doing that when you and Conner move to London?"

"Pardon?"

"Conner mentioned that you two are moving to London since he got a promotion at the firm and they're sending him overseas."

"Conner and I aren't together."

"What?" Her eyes widen, and I frown, not sure her surprise is genuine.

"He and I are no longer together." I quickly glance at May, finding her with her lips pressed together in a tight line. "I moved out weeks ago. We're getting divorced."

"Oh." Molly takes a step back and looks between May and me. "I had no idea. Conner told Brayden you've been staying at your parents' to help with your dad."

"I'm actually living in my brother's old place," I say, then thank my lucky stars when I spot our waiter headed our way with our cheese board.

"Sorry." He squeezes past Molly so he can place the wooden dish on the table between May and me. "Get my attention if you need anything else." He smiles at us.

"We will." I smile back, then look at Molly, who's stepped closer to Vanessa and Catharine. "We'll catch up soon," I lie, having no desire to talk to her or anyone else from my old life ever again.

"Yeah, sure." She nods, and I turn back to May, who keeps her attention across the room for a long moment before focusing on me.

"So, Conner hasn't told his friends that you two are getting divorced." She drops her gaze to the food between us as she grabs a piece of cheese and a few grapes.

"It would seem so." I sigh, picking up my glass to take a sip, needing the alcohol more now than I did before.

"I don't like that." Her concern-filled eyes lock on mine.

"Me neither." I rub my lips together, hoping like heck he will get it through his head that he and I are done and that there is no fricking way I am getting back with him.

Not even if doing so was the only way to guarantee the survival of the human race.

Chapter 7

Bridgett

Cookies

Parked outside the police station in the middle of town, I stare at the double doors while trying to convince myself to get out of the car. Last night, after drinks with May, I went home, showered, and got into bed. But after two hours of tossing and turning, I got up and went to the kitchen. The task of mixing up a new batch of cookie dough and then baking them was just what I needed to relax. By the time I had a couple dozen soft, golden cookies that looked magazine perfect, I was ready to sleep.

But now, with those cookies in a container on the seat next to me, I wonder why I didn't think about the fact that I would actually have to see Noah to give them to him.

"Maybe he's not even here," I mumble under my breath—hoping I'm right—before grabbing the plastic container, then forcing my hand to grasp the door handle and push it open. Once I'm out of my car, my knees feel weak, and my stomach churns as I walk across the sidewalk and up the steps to the precinct doors. Having never been to a police station before, I stand there for a second, not sure if I should knock or just go in. The option is taken away from me when a good-looking officer dressed in uniform opens the door.

"Hey, do you need some help?" he asks, his eyes roaming over me. I don't miss the fact that his attention lingers on my ring finger.

"I'm just dropping these off for Noah." I hold up the container, and his gaze moves to it before it meets mine once more.

"He's not here yet."

Halleluiah.

"Oh." I attempt to look disappointed. "Do you think I can leave these?"

"Sure, I'll put them on his desk if you want." He reaches out to take them, then holds up the clear container to look inside. "Did you make these?"

"I did."

"What's a guy gotta do to get homemade cookies?" he asks, and I can't help but smile.

"Take me to buy a car after working all night."

"Sheww." He whistles. "For a girl as pretty as you, I might do that."

"Benton, aren't you supposed to be heading out on patrol?" a deep voice barks, and my stomach bottoms out as I turn to find Noah walking up the sidewalk. He's wearing a baseball cap and dressed in a pair of dark jeans and a burnt-orange thermal that fits him like a second skin, with a duffle bag that looks about as big as me over his shoulder.

"I was on my way out," Benton answers, handing the container back to me. "Nice meeting you, miss."

"Yeah, you too." I bite my lip when he winks and swear I hear what sounds like a growl from Noah.

As Benton heads to the street, Noah stops on the stairs one step below me. With my heels on, we are just about eye-to-eye. With him not towering over me, I feel somewhat like we're on even ground, but it does nothing to ease the fluttering in my stomach that's only grown stronger since I heard his voice.

"What are you doing here?" he asks, and I realize I've just been staring at him, taking in the scruff on his jaw and how handsome he looks today.

"I made you cookies to say thank you for helping me out the other day." I hold out the container, but he doesn't take it or say a word. Instead, his eyes stay locked on mine, causing an uncomfortable knot to form in my stomach. "I figured nothing says *thank you* like baked goods." I rub my lips together, then continue rambling like an idiot to fill the silence. "They're chocolate chip... and not the cheap chocolate chips. The good ones from that fancy organic store across town." *Oh Lord, why did I say that?* "Not that there is anything wrong with the less-expensive ones. I just like the way the real stuff melts and tastes, so I feel like spending a couple of dollars more is worth it in the end. But the flour and stuff is all just from the regular store."

I push the container into his chest and let go, which forces him to grab it before it falls to the ground. "You can give them to your coworkers if you don't want them." I step around him and start down the steps, needing to get away, then gasp when his large palm wraps around my upper biceps.

"Where are you going?"

"To find the nearest lake to jump into." I hear him chuckle and tip my head his way, which is a mistake because I'm already attracted to him. Seeing him smile just makes that even more apparent. And that sucks because the last thing I need is to be crushing on him, especially when I'm very much still married, and he's so obviously not even a tad bit interested.

"Did you really make these?"

"I did," I tell him, then watch as he drops his duffle bag to the ground so he can open the container and take out one of the cookies. He places the entire thing into his mouth.

"Damn," he mumbles, closing his eyes while chewing, and I rub my lips together. I don't know what he looks like when he's having an orgasm, but the expression on his face now causes a rush of heat to spread up my neck to my cheeks. "And you're telling me they taste this good just because of some fancy chocolate?" he asks, opening his eyes and scanning my face.

"Um…mm-hmm." I clear my throat. "That and the mixture of butter and shortening I used."

"I'll have to get the recipe from you."

"I'll text it to Aiden and have him pass it along," I tell him as a very cute female officer pushes open the closed door. When his attention goes to her, his face lights up with a smile. As they begin talking, I descend to the sidewalk and start toward my car, needing to escape. Because the feeling of jealousy sitting in the pit of my stomach like a rotten apple is not an emotion I like much, even though it's very, very familiar.

"Bridgett," Noah calls out. I turn my head to look at him over my shoulder, finding his brows drawn together while the female officer watches me with a curious expression.

"I know you're working." I wave my hand. "I just wanted to drop those off. I'm sure I'll see you around." I give him a smile that feels totally awkward and forced. "Have a good night." I spin on my heel and hurry to my car, trying to make it look like I'm not rushing at all. Once inside, I start the engine, then back out of the space without sparing him another glance.

Instead of going home, I drive through town and head toward my parents' house. I put off going to check on my dad for a couple of days to avoid seeing my mom, but I can't do that any longer. I need to have a talk with him about my plans since my real-estate exam is coming up. If I pass, I hope to find a realtor I can learn the ropes from before stepping out completely on my own and quitting my job with his firm.

My dad owns one of the largest building companies in Tennessee, which his father passed down to him. He planned to have my brother take over when he retired, but Aiden fell in love with soccer, then went on to play professionally. He did that until a few months ago when he suffered an injury that took him out of the game for good. When my dad had a stroke that paralyzed him on one side of his body, Aiden came home to help out, and that's when he met his girlfriend, May. I don't know how long Aiden plans to help Dad, but I do know that my father is happier than he's been in a long time, having his son back in Tennessee and working right where he believes he was always supposed to be.

As I turn into my parents' driveway and the large house comes into view, I wonder what will happen to my childhood home if my parents divorce. Not that I have any fond memories attached to the residence I grew up that will make it difficult to let it go. But, still, it will be strange not to have both of them in one place.

After I park just around the bend in the circular driveway, I get out, walk to the front door, and don't bother knocking. Instead, I use my key to let myself in. It's quiet and dark inside, but I see light coming from the doorway of my dad's office at the end of the long hall and hear what sounds like people talking. When I get to the room, I find one of Dad's nurses sitting in a chair, and my dad in the hospital bed. They put it in the room after his stroke since it was too difficult for him to make it up the stairs. When his nurse's eyes meet mine, I smile, and she returns it before getting up and telling him she will be back in a bit with his dinner.

"Hey, Dad." I walk farther into the room, and he gives me a weary smile. One I'm sure is because my mother has probably been in a tizzy since he asked her for a divorce. I would not want to be a fly on the wall in this house any day of the week, but I definitely wouldn't want it now.

"Hey, you." He holds up one arm, and I walk to his bed, wrap my arms around him, and feel him embrace me. It makes my nose sting. For a while, I wasn't sure he would ever be back to his old self, but he's improved every week, and I have no doubt that he will be up and about doing all the things he did prior to his stroke before long. I just hope he doesn't go back to his old self completely; it's been nice actually being able to spend time with him.

He's been a workaholic all my life, and even if I understand it's necessary to work to earn a living, I also believe there should be a balance—especially when you have a family. With him working so much, we didn't go on vacations or have dinners together unless there was an event we were all required to attend. I'm sure his loyalty to his job also caused his relationship with my mom to suffer. I know it made *me* resent him in some ways.

"You doing okay?" he asks.

"Oh, yeah." I quickly dab my eyes with the sleeve of my sweater before straightening. "You look great. How are you feeling?"

"Better." His hand wraps around mine as I sit on the bed's edge. "I walked today."

"You did?" I flip my hand over so I can squeeze his fingers. "That's great news."

"It's progress." His eyes scan my face. "Now, tell me the truth. How are you really doing?"

"I'm okay." I shrug, not wanting him to worry about me. "I'm taking my realtor test the week after next."

"How do you feel about that?"

"Good. Ready." I rub my lips together. "If I pass, I plan on finding a realtor I can work with for a while until I feel comfortable enough to step out on my own."

"You could work at one of the properties with lots opening up and sell houses there to start," he offers, and my stomach churns. I would love to do that. I'd love to keep working for my dad and build a name for myself, but since I began working in his office, I've learned I'm not welcome. And right now, I don't have it in me to constantly tuck my tail between my legs and pretend the snide comments don't hurt.

"I think it might be better if I go somewhere else for a while. I don't want anyone mad at me for taking a job I haven't earned."

"You're my daughter. Bender and Sons is a family company. I'm not offering you a job as the CEO; I'm telling you that you can still work for the company. I *want* you to keep working for me." He shakes his head, his gaze going over my shoulder to the door, and a faraway look fills his eyes. "I know you working for me was never a part of your plan, just like it wasn't a part of Aiden's." His gaze comes back to me. "And I know it makes me a bastard for being happy that life has forced the two of you to come and work for me, but I am happy. So, if you came here today to tell me you're planning on quitting, I'm telling you that I do not accept your resignation. You'll get your license, work at one of the housing developments owned by Bender to learn the ropes, and then we'll go from there."

"Dad—"

"I love you, Bridgett," he cuts me off before I can tell him why I don't think that's a good idea. "I know I haven't said that enough, and I know I don't deserve anything from you, but please give me this."

The plea in his voice does me in, and I give in with a sigh. "Okay, Dad."

"Okay." His fingers squeeze mine. "Now, tell me what's going on with Conner. Has he signed the papers?" he asks, and I drag in a deep breath, then tell him everything that's happened, leaving out anything that might cause him stress, including any talk of Mom.

My mother might have wanted me to marry rich and stay that way, regardless of the emotional damage it might cause, but my dad did not, and he made it clear more than once that he did not like Conner. He even tried to talk me out of walking down the aisle on my wedding day, but hope blinded me, and I was convinced my story would be different than his.

I was obviously a fool with blinders on, but at least he's never said, "*I told you so.*"

When his nurse comes in with his dinner, I give him a kiss on the cheek and say goodbye to her before leaving and heading home. As I climb into bed, I don't think about the fact that I agreed to work for my dad, even though I'm not sure it's something I really want to do because I'm not sure I'll be able to change how the people working for him feel about me.

Instead, I dwell on my meeting with Noah and overthink every single second of it.

Chapter 8

Noah

I've Got a Room

Sitting in my squad car with my speed gun aimed up the road, I wait for someone to inevitably drive by going over the speed limit. Some get pissed that we have routine speed checks. But having had to console a woman whose daughter was killed by someone driving recklessly and witnessed firsthand the aftermath of a wreck that could have been avoided…. Yeah, I do not mind *one bit* that people get pissed when they're pulled over for breaking the law.

When a car comes around the bend, I glance down at the numbers that appear on the device, then set it aside and flip on my lights before pulling out behind them. As they start to pull over onto the shoulder of the road, the radio in my car cuts on, and Winnie who works at dispatch asks officers to respond to a fire at the townhomes where Bridgett lives.

With a curse, I speed by the car that has now pulled over and head into town, trying not to think about why the fuck a ball of some emotion I'm not ready to recognize is sitting heavy in my gut. When I arrive at the complex, the fire trucks are already set up in the lot, along with an ambulance and two other cruisers.

I notice right away they're focused on the building Bridgett's unit is in, but I don't see any flames coming from the structure, which connects three separate townhomes. There's only a plume of black smoke rising above the building, where they are aiming the water. I park at the curb and get out, doing a scan of the lot for Bridgett's car, but I don't find it in her designated parking space.

With it being after four in the evening on a Tuesday, its absence brings me some relief because it's likely she's not home right now and instead at work.

"Have you guys cleared Unit B?" I ask as I walk past the fire chief and the other officers gathered on the sidewalk.

"The building has been cleared," David, who's been the fire chief in town for the last year, shouts at my back. I still head for her doorway to check for myself. I knock and wait, then pound again. When I get no response, I head to the group of men gathered out front.

"You know someone who lives here?" David asks, and I jerk up my chin.

"My best friend's sister has been staying at his place." I look over at the ambulance and notice they have an older woman on a stretcher. "What happened?"

"Kitchen fire. The woman who lives in Unit A had a pan on the stove, and it caught on fire when she forgot about it and went to bed. She phoned in the fire when she noticed smoke filling her place. We were able to put it out, but…but there's currently a hole in the wall that gives a nice view into the unit next door, along with damage to the roof between the two homes." He glances at the building. "The building and units A through D will be uninhabitable for at least a couple of weeks. If you have your friend's number, you should let them know."

"Fuck." I jerk my cell out of my pocket and step away from the group as I dial Aiden. When he doesn't answer, I hang up and tap my cell against my thigh. I should have gotten Bridgett's number from her the first time I saw her. And I definitely should have gotten it when she shocked the shit out of me and showed up at my job with cookies.

Cookies that were so good I would have sworn she bought them if she hadn't been so adorable when talking about the kind of fucking chocolate chips she used.

Knowing I can't do anything right now but wait for her to show up, I get to work gathering the information I'll need to give to the families displaced by the fire.

At ten to six, when I watch Bridgett pull into the complex's parking lot, I get out of my car. With the lot now empty of all emergency personnel, she'll have no idea what took place today until she sees the yellow tape on her brother's front door. As she exits her car, I walk up behind her and try not to acknowledge how beautiful she looks with her hair up in a bun, and her fancy-ass clothes and shoes on.

"Bridgett," I call out. She spins around as a squeak of surprise escapes her lips currently painted a pretty burgundy color.

"Oh, you scared me." Her eyes move over my uniform. "What are you doing here? Are Aiden and May okay?"

"They're both fine—or I think they are. I haven't been able to get in touch with your brother all evening."

"I think he's been in meetings all day." She shakes her head as she pulls her handbag up over her shoulder. "Is everything okay?"

"Yes, and no." I rub my hand down my jaw rough with a thick layer of stubble. "There was a fire in the unit next to yours today."

"What?" she whispers, spinning around to look at the large structure. "Is everyone all right?"

"The woman who lives there went to the hospital for smoke inhalation but was released shortly after. No one else was home." She turns to face me. "That said, the building is uninhabitable and will be until the inspector can make it out, and the damage can be repaired."

"So I can't stay here?"

I shake my head, and my gut twists as her chin wobbles. "I got clearance from the chief to take you in to get your stuff."

"Okay." She drags in a deep breath. "Okay, sure, that would be great."

I lift my chin, then lead her up to her entryway, taking her key from her when I notice her hands shaking, making it difficult for her to unlock the door. I let us inside, then take my flashlight off my hip and flip it on. With it still being winter, it's dark even now.

"They shut the electricity off earlier as a precaution," I tell her, then hand her the light. "Lead the way."

She takes it and drops her bag onto the couch, shining the beam through the room and pausing in the kitchen, where the wall has a gaping black hole that looks like something out of a horror movie.

"Thank goodness no one was hurt," she says. I don't know if she's talking to me or herself.

"Are you going to stay with Aiden?"

"No." Her voice is quiet as we walk down the hall and enter her room. "I think there is a hotel just outside of town that does weekly rentals. Maybe I'll see if they have something available."

"You're not staying there," I bite out without thinking. I know the hotel she's talking about and answer the weekly calls we get from there when shit goes down. "What about your parents' place or Aiden's?"

"No." Her laugh is humorless. "My parents' place is not an option, and I know Aiden doesn't want me staying with him and May." She goes to the closet and comes out with a suitcase that she tosses up onto the bed a second later. Then she places the flashlight on the edge of the dresser, pointing it in the bed's direction. "I'll stay at that hotel."

"It's not safe."

"I'll be fine." She disappears into the closet again, and I hear the rattle of hangers before she comes back out with an armful of clothes, dumping them haphazardly into the bag before going back once more.

"I've got a room," I tell her when she comes out with another armful of stuff. "There isn't a bed, but there's a pull-out couch. You can crash on it until things get sorted and you can get back in here."

"That's very kind, but it's not necessary." I step forward to help her zip the bag.

"I know it's not necessary, but if you refuse to stay with your parents, Aiden, or me, I'm telling you now, I'll arrest you to keep you from staying at that hotel."

"You wouldn't!" She gasps, and I grin wickedly.

"Try me."

"You can't just arrest people. You need a reason." She goes back into the closet, grabbing another large suitcase.

"Yeah, but I know enough people that I could keep you there for a while before any real questions are asked."

"You're ridiculous," she huffs, going to the bathroom and taking the flashlight with her.

"You're staying with me." I scrub my hands over my head, knowing I'm setting myself up for disaster. I have a hard enough time keeping myself in check around her without her living under my roof, but here we fucking are. "I work a lot. We'll hardly see each other," I tell myself more than her.

"I don't want to impose."

"Just fucking accept my offer," I grit out and swear I hear her laugh.

"Okay, if you're sure you don't mind."

"I don't." I watch her come out with a small bag that looks like a purse, along with shower shit, a curling iron, and a blow-dryer. She puts it all into the bag, then picks up a laundry basket from the floor, turns it upside down, and dumps the contents in there, as well.

I ignore the fact that it's all lacy shit in a multitude of colors.

"Okay, I think that's everything I need for now." She looks around.

"I'm sure I can get you back in here if you need anything else," I assure her.

"I'll need to borrow your washer. Everything smells like smoke."

"I don't have one." I keep my face blank, and she blinks at me. "I'm just kidding. That's fine." I close her second bag. "Do you wanna bring your pillow?"

"Yeah." She grabs it off the bed, along with the thick blanket. I haul both bags down the hall to the front door, and she stops to get her purse before following me outside.

When she pops the trunk of her car, I put the luggage inside, then take the stuff in her arms and put it in with them before slamming it closed and turning to face her. "You can follow me to my place. I'll get you settled, then take off."

"Are you on the clock right now?"

"Yeah."

She shakes her head and takes a step back. "I can find somewhere to hang out until you're off tonight."

"Babe, I'm not off until four a.m." I open her door.

"Noah."

"Just follow me." I slam her door and head for my car without a backward glance, waiting until she's at the entrance of the parking lot before pulling out in front of her.

It takes fifteen minutes to get out of town. When I hit the dirt road that leads to my house, I check the rearview mirror, finding Bridgett right behind me. I park in front of my double garage, open the door with the push of a button, then roll down the window and wave her in.

A few minutes later, carrying her luggage, I stop at the front door and glance down at Bridgett on the step below me. "Brace, babe. Lola is gonna be excited someone new is here, but she's also on edge with her puppies in the house."

"There are puppies in the house?" she breathes like I just told her Santa is real and we're taking a trip to the North Pole to visit him.

"Yeah." I grin, then push open the door. As soon as I do, Lola rushes to greet me. Her tail wags a mile a second before she goes on alert and begins to bark. "Lola, calm." I drop the bags and pick her up, then turn to face Bridgett, who looks a mixture of scared and in love.

"She's very sweet. You just have to show her you're not someone she needs to be afraid of," I tell her. Bridgett carefully reaches out her hand to Lola, allowing the pup to smell her fingers before petting the top of her head.

"She's cute. What kind of dog is she?"

"My best guess is a mixture of Pomeranian and poodle, but really, I don't know. I found her at an abandoned house a few months ago."

"And she had puppies?"

"Just had them a couple of weeks ago. That was a surprise I found out about when I took her to the vet for the first time." I carry her into the house, leaving the bags in the hall. When I get to the laundry room, I place Lola down, and she immediately goes to the box where her three pups are rooting around, looking for her.

"They are so tiny," Bridgett whispers, stepping up behind me and pressing her tits into my arm.

"They are." I watch Lola lie down for them to feed, then point out the washer and dryer. "This is the laundry." I leave the room, then head farther down the hall to the kitchen. "Eat and drink anything you want." I point at the stairs. "My room is up there." I head across the living room and open the door to my spare bedroom that is more office than anything else. "The couch folds out into a bed, and there are sheets and blankets in the closet." I turn to face her and find her looking around the room. "I hate to leave you like this, but I gotta get back into town. My boys are covering for me now, but—"

"Please, don't apologize," she cuts me off. "You're doing me a huge favor by letting me stay here."

"It's not a big deal." I head out of the room, and she follows me to where I stop in the kitchen. "I'm gonna leave you my cell number. If you need anything, just call." I jot down my digits on the pad of paper on the counter. "Are you working tomorrow?"

"Yeah."

"I might see you in the morning." I go to the junk drawer and dig through until I find a spare key and a clicker for the garage door. "If I'm passed out by the time you get up, you can use these to come and go whenever you want."

"Thanks," she whispers, and I lift my chin.

"Call your brother and let him know what's going on."

"I will," she assures me, then rubs her lips together as she wraps her arms around her middle. Seeing her looking so vulnerable makes my insides twist with the urge to give her a hug, but I remind myself it's not my place to comfort her.

"I'll set the alarm before I leave."

"Okay." She nods. And with that, I force myself to walk away.

Chapter 9

Bridgett

Relief

Blinking my eyes open, I hear the television's low volume coming through the wall while the smell of bacon permeates the air around me. I drag in a deep breath and let it out slowly. Noah is safe and just on the other side of the door.

It's odd to feel so relieved that he made it home. I never once worried about Conner while he was out or even gone for weeks, traveling for business. But every night, even the nights before the one I just spent under Noah's roof, I've thought about him, wondered if he was okay, and hoped I didn't wake up to some story on the news about an officer either injured or killed in the line of duty.

Grabbing my pillow, I drag it over my head and groan. My feelings for him have grown wildly out of control. Even reminding myself that I need to keep my emotions in check isn't working.

Last evening, when he offered me a room at his place, I wanted to keep refusing him. But the truth is, I needed the lifeline he tossed my way. I might have enough money to get a room at a seedy hotel for a week, but I'd likely be sleeping in my car after that. I couldn't ask my brother and May if I could stay with them, even knowing they would probably feel bad for me and allow it.

Which I confirmed when I called Aiden to tell him what happened, and May suggested I stay at their place in her guest room.

No.

And I'd rather jump off a cliff than ask my parents if I could stay with them. My dad wouldn't be difficult to deal with if he were on his own, but he's *not*. And my mother would, without a doubt, use the situation as a reason to dig in her heels about why I should go back to Conner.

As the steady beep of my alarm begins to sound, I come out of my thoughts and toss my pillow away, then grab my phone off the floor to shut it off. I get up and fold my blankets, placing them on the arm of the couch, then put on my robe and grab my bathroom stuff before going to the door. With a deep breath, I step out into the living room and am instantly relieved when I don't see Noah there or in the kitchen, making it easier for me to avoid him for a little longer. After a quick shower, I apply my makeup, which doesn't take long since the task is one I have been doing almost every day since I was fifteen.

Ready—or mostly ready, anyway—I leave the bathroom, taking my stuff with me, and stop dead in my tracks when I spot Noah and the female officer he had been happy to see days ago when I brought him the cookies. The two of them hold coffee mugs as they talk quietly in the kitchen.

My stomach sinks to my toes, and I instantly hate how perfect they look together. Both of them are dressed in workout gear that shows off just how in shape they are. Really, they look like they belong on one of those ads for CrossFit or Body Boot Camp. Meanwhile, I've been eating my feelings for weeks and have gained not just weight in my stomach but also in my bottom and hips.

Not that I minded until this moment.

"Morning," the woman says, and I snap out of my pity party for one and plaster a smile on my face.

"Morning," I greet her, then look down when I feel paws on my calf, finding Lola standing on her hind legs. "Hey, sweet girl." My smile is genuine as I lean down to rub the top of her head. She was a little leery of me after Noah left last night, but by the time I was finished with my laundry, we were the best of friends.

"You want some breakfast, babe?" Noah asks, and my stomach twists at his deep voice. Every time he's called me *babe* in the past, it's made my heart beat a little funny. Now, I know it's just a nickname he's probably given to dozens of women.

"I wish, but I don't have time. I'm actually running late since I need to be at the office a little earlier today," I lie as I straighten from petting Lola, then toss a smile in his direction but avoid eye contact. "Be back." I head to my room to get dressed.

When I'm done, I grab my purse and phone and step into the living room to find Noah and the woman still in the kitchen. Since I can't avoid them, I head their way. Both of their gazes come to me.

"I didn't get to introduce myself the other day or this morning," the woman says as soon as I step into the room. "I'm Jennifer. Noah and I used to be partners." She holds out her hand, and I grab hold of it on instinct.

"Nice to meet you. I'm Bridgett. Noah and my brother are best friends. That's why I'm here." I add the last part, wanting to make sure she knows why I'm staying with her boyfriend.

"He mentioned that." She glances over at him and smirks. "And just so you know, he and I aren't together. He just enjoys torturing me with weekly workouts."

Wait, what?

I clear my throat, and she gives me a knowing smile.

"Here," Noah says as she lets my hand go. I drop my eyes to the black travel mug he's holding toward me. "I made bacon. If you want, I'll make a sandwich you can take with you."

"Thank you." I take the mug, feeling like the biggest kind of ass. "That's not necessary. I'll just get something to eat at a drive-thru on my way through town."

"Bridgett, if a man offers to make you food, you accept," Jennifer informs me, and I rub my lips together.

"I guess I could eat a bacon sandwich," I say quietly, and she laughs while I hear Noah grunt. Taking my coffee with me, I step back toward the counter and set down my bag while Noah goes to the fridge and pulls out mayo and cheese.

"Did you call your brother last night?" he asks as he plops the stuff in his hand on the counter.

"I did. He said he would talk to the people he was renting from and figure out what's going to happen, then let me know."

"Sorry to hear about your place," Jennifer says as she hops up onto one of the counters like she's been here often and it's something normal for her to do.

"Thanks." I fiddle with the handle of the coffee mug I'm still clutching, and my eyes go to Noah. I watch his biceps flex as he slathers mayo on two pieces of bread.

"Noah mentioned you work for Bender and Sons," she prompts, and I drag my gaze off Noah to look at her.

"I do."

"You guys are building my girlfriend's and my house."

"Really?"

"Yeah, it's in the new subdivision just outside of Franklin." She takes a sip of coffee.

"That's a beautiful area," I say, knowing exactly what she's talking about.

"It really is," she agrees, then glances at Noah. "I keep telling this guy he needs to look into building over there."

"Why?" I blurt without thinking. I mean, I'm not sure if Noah owns this house, but I can honestly say I loved it the moment we pulled onto the property last night.

I thought he'd have an apartment in town or some other kind of bachelor pad, but I was pleasantly surprised by the tree-covered lot and cute little house tucked into the middle of the woods that reminded me of something out of a storybook. And the inside is just as beautiful as the outside, with timeless fixtures and an open floorplan that would be perfect for entertaining or a growing family.

"Well, if he doesn't get the job as detective in town, Franklin will be an easier commute for him to get into Nashville," she says, and I look over at Noah.

"When will you know if you got the position?" I ask, and he meets my gaze.

"Next week."

"They should have already told him." She huffs. "I mean, no offense to the other guys who've applied, but none of them deserve it like Noah does."

I nod because I'm sure she's right.

"If it's meant to be, it will happen." Noah sighs as he picks up the sandwich he made for me and wraps it in a paper towel. "And I'm not moving unless you can find me at least three acres in Franklin for under five hundred thousand."

"Since I paid that for my postage-stamp-sized lot, you know that's never going to happen."

"Then I guess I'm never moving," he mutters to her while handing me my sandwich, his eyes locking with mine. "What time do you normally get home from work in the evenings?"

"It depends, but usually around five."

"I'll be at work when you get here."

"Okay."

"Let me see your phone," he orders. I set my coffee down and dig through my bag for my cell, then hand it to him after unlocking the screen. A few seconds later, after he's done doing whatever it is he's doing, his phone on the counter begins to ring. "All right." He hands my cell back to me. "I'll send you a text with the code for the alarm and instructions on how to disarm it when you get back here tonight. Just make sure you arm it when you're inside and locked in."

"I will." I place my phone back into my purse and grab my coffee. "I guess I'll see you tomorrow?"

"Yeah." He lifts his chin but doesn't take his eyes off mine. I shift on my heels, then drop my gaze and step around him, glancing at Jennifer. "It was nice meeting you."

"You too." She smiles, then looks between Noah and me and shakes her head. "I'm sure I'll see you around."

I nod, figuring she's right, then hustle out of the kitchen and walk down the hall and out the door. Once I'm in my car, I toss my purse onto the passenger seat, place my coffee in the cupholder, then grab my keys to start the engine. I stop when someone taps on my window. I turn my head and come face-to-face with Noah, noticing he's holding the key and clicker for the garage door he left on the counter last night.

"Crap." I shake my head and hit the button for the window to roll it down. "Sorry, I totally forgot."

"You would have realized eventually." He clips the clicker onto my visor, then hands me the key while locking his gaze with mine and asking softly, "Are you doing okay?"

"Yeah," I whisper, not sure why that quietly asked question makes my throat tight, but it does.

"All right." He stands back and taps the roof of my car. "I'll see you tomorrow, babe."

"See you tomorrow." I muster up a smile, then hit the button for the garage, which sends the door up. I back out and do a three-point turn in the yard since there isn't an actual driveway, then glance in the rearview mirror and notice he hasn't moved from his position. And he doesn't until I'm almost halfway down the road.

And darn it all, my stupid heart flutters in my chest because I know I'll see him again tomorrow.

Chapter 10

Bridgett

Hell No

Sitting on the floor in the laundry room, I giggle as Lola's puppies—who I've named Coco, Louie, and Chanel—attempt to waddle around me with their eyes barely open. I had no idea they could get any cuter, but as they gain weight and become more active, they do. And if there was a way I could convince Noah to keep them all, I would. But he's already told me he's only keeping Chanel. A couple of people he works with are adopting the other two.

Hearing the back door that leads to the garage open, my nerves start to buzz. Today, both Noah and I have the day off, which means I can't avoid him—something I've gotten very good at doing.

"You still in here with them?" He stops in the doorway and crosses his arms over his chest as he watches me, making me feel self-conscious, especially since the only thing I did today was brush my teeth and tie my hair up into a bun. It doesn't help that he looks ready to break hearts, even in sweats and a hoodie, with a backward ball cap on his head.

"I can't help it. They are so cute." I pick up the puppy closest to me and kiss the top of its furry head. "When I move out, I might just tuck one of them in my bag." I smile as he laughs, then ask, "What were you doing outside?"

"Just cleaning up some of the leaves and shit from the gardens since the weather is warming up."

"Do you want some help?"

"No, I'm just about done. I was only coming in for a garbage bag."
He lets his arms fall to his sides, then looks down the hall. "Are you
cooking?"

"I put on a pot of Guinness stew."

"Smells good." He taps the edge of the door before walking off.
Since there is no way I'll just sit on my butt and not help him, I carefully
place all three puppies back in the box with Lola, who's been snoozing as
I babysat, then get up off the floor. With Noah in the kitchen digging
under the sink, I head to my room and put on a sweater and boots, then
grab my vest out of the closet. I walk out of my room, and as soon as his
eyes lock on me, he frowns.

"Where are you going?"

"To help you." I walk to where he's standing and take the garbage
bags out of his hand. "Is that okay?"

"I'm guessing if I say no, you'll ignore me, so sure." He looks me
over, then shakes his head. "Do you have a hat?"

"No, but I don't think I need one."

"Babe, it's cold. Come on." He places his hand against my lower
back, then leads me down the hall, letting his palm fall away as he goes
into the laundry room. "You can use this." He comes back a second later
and starts to place his navy-blue beanie on my head, then stops. "You
need to take your hair down," he mumbles. Then, with a flick of his wrist,
my hair comes tumbling out of the bun I had it in, and he places his
police-issued hat on my head.

"Thanks," I mumble, fixing my hair as his eyes roam over my face.

"Sure." He takes a step back away from me, then turns to head down
the hall and opens the door. When we get outside, we go to the front of
the house where *not* a small but a *huge* pile of leaves and yard debris waits.

"You can help by holding the bag." He walks around me to the
mound, and I open the bag for him, then look at the driveway when I
hear a car. With the trees scattered throughout the yard, it takes a second
to see the vehicle, but when I spot a black Mercedes, my stomach pitches.

"Oh my God," I whisper, my mind going a million miles an hour as
Conner parks his car in the middle of the dirt driveway.

"Tell me that's not your fucking ex," Noah rumbles, and I turn to
face him. The minute our gazes lock, his eyes scan mine, and the look he
gives me sends a chill down my spine. "Go in the house."

"Bridgett!" Conner yells. I glance his way, finding him already
halfway across the yard.

"Not fucking happening." Noah steps in front of me and barks out,

"Get back in your car."

"I want to talk to my wife." Conner holds up his hands, then locks his eyes on mine. "Please, Bridgett, I just want to talk."

"How did you know I was here?" I ask, and Noah turns to pin me with a glare.

"Your mom told me," Conner says, and my spine stiffens. I shouldn't be surprised she would tell him where I was, but that doesn't mean it doesn't bother me.

"Bud, get back in your car and get off my property."

"You can't tell me what to—"

"Go home, Conner," I cut him off. "I told you the last time you sent me a text that we have nothing to talk about. That still stands."

"I want you to move home. I want you back, Bridgett. I'm tired of this game."

"This isn't a game." I shake my head while my hands ball into fists.

"Babe, get inside," Noah says softly while catching my gaze. I nod, feeling exhausted all of a sudden.

"Babe?" Conner yells as I start to walk toward the garage. "What the fuck is that, Bridgett? You didn't want to put out for me, but you're putting out for *this* douche?" He laughs without humor, and anger mixed with embarrassment twists in my stomach. "I shouldn't be surprised you'd spread your legs for a place to live."

I spin around to tell him to go fuck himself but snap my mouth shut when I find Noah shoving him back toward his car, causing him to stumble. He shoves him again every time Conner rights himself.

"You come near her again, I'll arrest you," Noah snarls as he shoves him one last time, sending him flying onto the hood of his Mercedes.

"Fuck you, man!" Conner roars, jerking upright and kicking his foot like a kid throwing a fit, causing rocks to fly out. "And fuck that stupid bitch." He storms to the driver's side door and rips it open. A moment later, his engine starts, and a second after that, he backs out of the driveway, going way too fast, causing his tires to squeal as he spins around the corner.

With my arms wrapped around my middle, I watch Noah's hands flex and his back rise and fall. Even without seeing his face, I know he's angry, and I know that it's because of me. "I'm sorry," I call out, and his shoulders jerk. "I'll find somewhere else to stay."

"You're not fucking leaving, Bridgett." He turns to face me. "But I do want you to talk to your lawyer and tell him what happened." He prowls my way. "Are you okay?"

"No." I shake my head, then drag in a deep breath. "I hate him."

"I can understand why." He stops in front of me. "Your mom told him you were staying here."

"She must have found out from Aiden." I swallow, trying to ignore the fact that my throat aches and my nose is starting to sting.

"You didn't tell her?"

"I haven't spoken to her for a couple of weeks." My chin wobbles.

"Please don't cry," he says softly, and I shake my head.

"I won't." As soon as the lie slips past my lips, a tear slides down my cheek.

"Fuck, baby." He drags me against him and cups the back of my head with his large palm. "Let it out."

I want to. I want to let all the anger, sadness, and resentment that has been sitting on my chest for weeks loose, but I can't because I don't know what will happen if I let myself feel the full force of those emotions.

"I'm okay." I step out of his hold and swipe away the tears still wet on my cheeks.

"Bridgett." My name is soft, and I shake my head as I turn my back to him.

"We should finish cleaning up. The sun will be setting soon." I walk to the black garbage bag and pick it up off the ground where I dropped it, shaking it out. It feels like forever before he moves, but when he does, he doesn't say another word. Nor do I. Then again, what is there to say?

Chapter 11

Bridgett

Simple

Sitting at the counter in Noah's kitchen, I nibble my bottom lip as I answer the third to last question on my official realtor licensing exam. As my palms begin to sweat, I click on one of the multiple-choice answers I think fits best, then move on to the next question and the next.

On the last and final one, I hold my breath as I click on my answer…and then close my eyes after the screen changes and it says I passed. The relief I feel causes tears to fill my eyes instantly, and I cover my face as I start to cry.

I've felt like I've been trying to swim upstream in a raging river for weeks, and each time I'm sure I've grabbed hold of something solid that will allow me to get to shore, a wave crashes into me, sending me under all over again. But with this, I've finally got something that will one day lead to me being completely independent. I won't need anyone to take care of me ever again.

"What the fuck happened?" Noah barks, and I uncover my face and find him standing in the entryway to the kitchen, dressed in a suit—something I never imagined seeing him in because who the heck would make one in his size?

"Nothing." I sniffle, using the sleeve of my sweater to dry the tears on my cheeks. Not that it actually helps since tears continue slipping from between my lashes.

"You're crying, so something happened." He comes around the

counter to where I'm sitting and then spins my computer around so he can look at the screen. "What is this?" His eyes lock on mine, and I shake my head as I swallow.

"It's…it's my realtor test." I wipe my cheeks again. "I just took it and found out I passed."

As he studies me, I shift on the stool. Since the day Conner showed up here, things between Noah and I have been awkward, and I no longer know if it's him avoiding me or me avoiding him.

"You took a test to become a realtor?" He looks at the screen again before focusing on me once more.

"Yeah."

"You never mentioned you were doing that."

"It's not a big deal."

"Babe, it's a big fucking deal." He straightens and begins to loosen the tie around his neck.

"Why are you so dressed up?" I eye him as he takes off his suit jacket and places it on the back of one of the barstools.

"I had a meeting with my captain." He moves into the kitchen and goes to the pantry.

"Wait, did you find out if you made detective today?" I ask, getting off my stool to follow him.

"I did."

"And?" I watch as he comes out of the pantry, holding a bottle of very expensive champagne covered in a layer of dust.

"I got the promotion," he says, so casually I would assume it doesn't mean anything to him that he got the job he's been vying for. But I know that's not true.

"Oh my God." I rush him and wrap my arms around his waist, resting the side of my head against his chest. "I'm so happy for you." I tip my head back and find his chin dipped and his gaze soft. "I had no doubt you would get the job." I smile. "Are you happy?"

"Yeah," he mutters, and I realize where I am and that he might not want me wrapped around him like a boa constrictor. Letting him go, I step back and rub my palms down the front of the leggings I put on when I got home from work this evening.

"Sorry, I'm just happy for you," I say. His eyes roam over me from head to toe before he clears his throat and holds up the bottle of champagne between us.

"I'm sure this tastes like shit, but a friend bought it for a special occasion."

"That champagne is one of the best on the market. It does not taste like crap," I inform him, and he laughs, the deep, rumbling sound making my belly feel funny. "Give it to me before you ruin it with your negative energy."

I take it from his hand and then grab a rag to wipe it down before starting the task of carefully removing the black-and-gold metal foil around the cork and unscrewing the casing over the top.

When I'm done, I hand it back to him, noticing he now has the first button of his shirt undone and the sleeves rolled up, exposing his throat and muscular forearms. "Here, you can pull out the cork."

Taking it from me, he places his thumb under the edge, and my eyes widen. "Wa—!" I open my mouth to tell him not to open it like that, but I'm too late. The cork flies out, cracking against the ceiling in the kitchen, and champagne bubbles out from the bottle, spilling onto the tile at our feet. "You just twist it off," I whisper, and he looks at me before his eyes go to the very obvious indent in the ceiling above us, then to his feet. "I'll clean it up."

"I got it. You can pour." He hands me the bottle, then grabs some paper towels to clean up the floor.

"Do you have champagne glasses?" I ask, and the moment he looks at me, I know that's a dumb question because the guy doesn't even have matching drinkware. "Never mind."

I go to the cabinet where he keeps his glasses and coffee mugs and grab two of them. Then, unwilling to drink warm champagne, no matter if it is some of the best out there, I go to the freezer, get some ice cubes, and put a few in each of our cups before pouring the clear bubbly.

By the time I've got each of us a glass, he's done with the task of cleaning up the floor. I hand him his drink, then hold up mine. "To you becoming a detective."

"And to you passing your realtor test." He touches his cup to mine, and our eyes lock as we take a drink. For me, the bubbly liquid hits my tongue, making me want more. But he obviously does not feel the same, which he makes very clear by the expression of disgust on his handsome face.

"Fuck, how can you drink that shit?" he asks, wiping his mouth with the back of his hand.

"It's delicious." I giggle, taking another sip while he shakes his head and sets his cup down.

"It's garbage." He goes to the fridge, grabs a bottle of some dark liquid from the cabinet above it, then looks back at me. "So, what's your plan now that you've got your realtor license?" He pours himself two fingers of whiskey.

"I was going to work under a realtor, but my dad wants me to work for Bender and Sons as a realtor at one of the properties he owns." I lean against the counter behind me, my body already feeling relaxed from the little bit of champagne I've had.

"What do *you* want?" he asks, leaning his hip against the counter opposite me.

I drag in a breath as I think about how to respond to that question. "I don't know," I answer truthfully. "I like the idea of working for my family's business, but I don't want anyone thinking I haven't earned whatever job I'm given." I lift one shoulder.

"Someone made you feel like that?" he asks, once again studying me. For once, I don't feel uncomfortable, probably thanks to the alcohol filling my empty stomach.

"Everyone in my dad's office hates me." I laugh before taking another sip of my drink, and he gives me a doubtful look. "It's true. I've overheard them talking about me more than once. None of them wants me there, and none of them thinks I should be there regardless of the fact that my dad owns the company."

"What the fuck?"

"I don't blame them." I wave a hand out between us. "I have a degree in business that I never used, and until my dad gave me a job, I never worked a day in my life. If I were someone who walked in off the street applying for the position I have, even if it is just secretarial work, they wouldn't have hired me."

"That might be so, babe, but them talking shit about you is fucked up."

"It doesn't matter." I turn to pour myself another cupful of champagne, this one much fuller than the last. "My dad wants me to keep working for him. And, honestly, I like the idea." I turn back toward him. "I don't know what will happen with Aiden once Dad is back on his feet, but if he leaves and I stop working there, the business will likely be turned over to the board, and I don't want that. I know how much the company means to my father and what it meant to my grandfather, and none of the people my dad has on the board are emotionally invested in the success or failure of the business."

"So you want to run the company?"

"No. Absolutely not." My nose scrunches. "My dad was never around when I was growing up, and someday when I find the right guy, I want to have kids and focus on the whole Mom thing."

"You wanna be a soccer mom?"

"If my kids are in soccer, sure." I smile, and he chuckles. "I just want to be available if my children need me, and running a company like my dad's wouldn't allow me to do that." I let out a breath. "Honestly, I just want a simple life. I want to make enough money to support myself so I never have to depend on another man again. I also don't want my job to be my entire existence."

"I get that," he says quietly, then looks at my stomach when it growls loudly. "Hungry?"

"Yes, I didn't eat today because I was nervous about what would happen when I took the test."

"Let's get you some food." He grabs his cell out of the pocket of his suit. "How does pizza sound for dinner?"

"Good, but I'm buying."

"Not happening," he denies instantly, and I narrow my eyes. Since I've been staying here, he hasn't let me give him any money, and the only way I've been able to help out is by picking up groceries when I see things are running low—and he made it clear that he doesn't even want me doing that.

I've found cash tucked into my purse that I know I didn't put there more than once or found money on the counter with a note labeled: *Grocery Money*. Each and every time, I've given it back to him by leaving it somewhere he would eventually find it. But that hasn't stopped him from continuing to be high-handed when it comes to paying.

"I want to pay."

"Next time," he mumbles, focusing his attention on his cell. "What kind of pizza do you want?"

"You know, you're really annoying."

"Yep." He looks up from his phone. "Now, what kind of pizza do you want?"

"Everything."

"My kind of girl." He grins, and my belly flips.

As he places the pizza order, I head into the living room, needing a minute to get myself together because him saying that I'm his kind of girl makes me feel things I should not be feeling. He's my brother's best friend and the guy who was nice enough to let me stay with him, nothing more.

Not to mention, I'm still technically married and should not even be interested in someone else. I mean, there must be a time limit on how long you have to wait after a divorce to start lusting after another man. And with Conner still dragging his feet regarding signing the divorce papers, it will likely be a few more weeks before that clock starts ticking.

"What are you thinking about?" Noah walks into the living room after getting off his phone.

"When I can start dating again," I answer without thought, then cringe. "Not that I'm interested in anyone. I was just wondering when a person would do something like that," I blabber. He sits on the couch next to me, not on the other side of the sofa where he *should* be.

"Whenever you're ready." He leans his head back against the cushion and closes his eyes.

"What?"

"You should start dating whenever you feel ready. There isn't a time limit." He stretches out his long legs, and when his thigh rubs against mine, I bring my knees to my chest.

"I'm still married."

"You don't have a ring on your finger." He rolls his head my way and pins me with a stare. "You going back to your ex?"

"Absolutely not."

"That's what I thought." His gaze drops to my mouth for the briefest of seconds, causing my heart to pound. "Life is way too fucking short to live on someone else's timeline, babe. Do whatever the fuck makes you happy."

"As simple as that?"

"As simple as that." He holds my stare, and I nod. Maybe he's right. Perhaps I need to stop caring what other people think and just live my life in whatever way makes me happy.

Chapter 12

Noah

Cherries

I watch Bridgett as she sleeps with her head on the armrest of the couch, her hair down around her shoulder, and her cheeks pink from the champagne she drank. Even passed-out drunk, she's adorable. Actually, she's adorable all the time, which has become a problem. When I didn't know her as anything more than Aiden's little sister, it was easy to brush off my attraction to her. *Now, not so much.* Whenever I'm around her, the urge to kiss her or touch her is almost unbearable.

I want her. I want to know what she tastes like. Want to know if her skin is as soft as it looks. And I want to know what sounds she'll make when I go down on her or fuck her. And all of that would be easy enough to get over, but I don't *just* want to fuck her. I've grown protective of her and have come to crave her presence. She's a mystery I want to solve, but with her being so skittish around me, it's almost impossible to figure her out.

That said, I've figured out that her family has not looked out for her, including my best friend, which is probably why she ended up married to a man like her ex. I've learned that she's got a soft heart, she's funny even when she's not trying to be, and she's afraid of not earning her place, no matter where that is. I didn't expect to like her, not when we come from such vastly different backgrounds, but I do. And I honestly don't know what to do with that.

I told her this evening that life is too short to live on someone else's timeline, but I'm not sure I could take my advice when it comes to her. She's still not divorced from the dick she married, and even if I know she's attracted to me, I'm not sure taking advantage of that would be the right move. Going too fast could blow up in my face, but waiting until I think she might be ready could cause its own set of problems.

My jaw shifts, and my hands ball into fists. I've always been one to look at a situation and figure out the right move, but I'm at a loss for what to do when it comes to her.

Knowing I won't be able to figure that shit out tonight, I push up off the couch, then start to pick her up so I can put her to bed. Her eyes open as her hands move to my chest.

"Noah."

"Just putting you to bed, babe," I tell her softly, lifting her off the couch. She makes a sound of protest in the back of her throat before shaking her head.

"I can walk."

I ignore her and carry her to her room, hitting the light switch with my elbow, which turns on the desk lamp, casting a soft glow around the office. Since she's been staying here, I haven't come into her space, but seeing it now causes something to shift inside my chest. Her suitcases are both open on the floor with her clothes neatly packed inside like she's just waiting to close them up and leave, and the couch looks like she's never pulled out the bed.

"Have you been sleeping on the couch?" I ask, placing her on the cool leather loveseat. She tips her head back to look at me.

"Yes."

"Babe, what the fuck?"

"It's comfortable." She pulls the blanket she brought with her off the back and lays her head on her pillow, closing her eyes. "You shouldn't have let me drink so much champagne."

"I tried to cut you off, but you told me you couldn't let it go to waste."

"Oh, yeah," she murmurs, and I bite back a grin.

"You'll feel better in the morning."

"That's doubtful. Champagne hangovers are the worst." She tucks the blanket up around her neck, and I shake my head, then go to the closet to grab a thicker one before spreading it over her. "Thank you."

"We're gonna have a talk tomorrow."

"About what?" She peeks one eye open to look at me.

"About you not unpacking." I lean over and tuck a piece of hair behind her ear, watching up close as her nose scrunches. "Get some sleep." I stand back, then go to the door and cut the light before leaving the room.

It takes me a few minutes to close everything down and get the house locked up, and even longer to fall asleep after I get into bed.

The next morning, standing in the kitchen with a cup of coffee in hand, I look toward Bridgett's bedroom door. When it opens, I smile as she mumbles, "Morning," before ducking her head and rushing to the bathroom across the room with her arms full.

A couple of seconds later, I hear the shower turn on, so I wait a few minutes before tossing one of the breakfast sandwiches she eats—unless I cook—into the microwave. I then pour her a cup of coffee, adding the vanilla creamer she always uses. Knowing she's probably hungover, I grab a bottle of Tylenol from the cupboard and place it next to a glass of water on the island, along with her sandwich and coffee before grabbing a set of keys off the hook near the back door and heading outside.

When I get down the steps off the deck, I go to where my four-wheeler is parked under a slanted roof attached to the house and hook up the trailer, then straddle the seat and start the engine. After turning around in the yard, I drive down the overgrown path that leads to the backside of the property and hope like fuck the single-wide trailer I lived in for two years before building my house wasn't damaged this winter.

When it comes into view, I scan the roof for any branches that might have fallen off the surrounding trees but find none. I park and get off, then head inside. The interior is still in good shape, and I know that even if I have no desire to be a landlord, I could easily rent the space out for a thousand or more dollars a month.

Hell, Bridgett could even move in here and be comfortable, but I don't like the idea of her being back here on her own.

Or, if I'm honest, I just don't like the idea of her being so far away from me.

Bypassing the kitchen, I head to the back bedroom and stop in the doorway. When my house was completed four years ago, I bought all new furniture first because I barely fit the queen bed I had been sleeping on for a couple of years. But also because most of the things I owned were hand-me-downs, and it was time to replace them all. I planned on donating the old stuff but decided to wrap everything in plastic and leave it in the trailer in case someone else needed it at some point. I'm glad I did.

When I'm done getting the wooden bedframe broken down, and it and the mattress and box spring out of the room and onto the trailer, I head back to the house. I park the ATV at the bottom of the steps, then take the headboard inside, noticing a slip of paper on the counter and the dishwasher running. Picking up the note, I scan the frilly writing.

Thank you for breakfast. Ran out to do some errands. Be back soon. xx

Seeing the Xs at the bottom scribbled over, I shake my head and bite back a smile. I lean the headboard I'm still holding against one of the walls, then bring everything else inside and get to work.

"Umm...what is going on?" Bridgett asks. I pause just below the landing of the stairs, the couch balancing on its arm since the only way to get it up to the second floor alone is to push it end-over-end.

"I'm taking the couch upstairs."

"Is this your way of telling me you're kicking me out?"

"No. This is my way of telling you that you're not sleeping on a couch while under this roof." I drop my gaze to the bags she's holding. "You went to the grocery store?"

"I got stuff to make blueberry scones and lasagna for dinner."

"Babe, if you keep feeding me cookies and shit, I'm gonna have a heart attack running after a perp."

"Don't say that!" She gasps.

"It's the truth."

"You don't have to eat what I cook."

"I don't, but I'm also not going to pass up your cooking." I tip the couch up the stairs.

"Well, then—" She lifts her chin ever so slightly while crossing her arms over her ample chest. "I guess it's good you're a fancy detective now, and it's someone else's job to run after the bad guys."

"I guess it is." I squat, then stand, hefting the couch up and over one more time.

"Do you want me to help?"

"Fuck, no." I groan, flipping the couch again, which places it at the top of the stairs on the second floor. As I begin pushing it down the short hall and into the small sitting area with the reading nook I never use, I hear her footsteps on the stairs. A second later, she's at my side, bent at the waist with her hands on the armrest, helping me push. "I thought I said I didn't need your help."

"And all I heard was blah, blah, blah."

"Smartass." I turn to look at her and catch her smile, which means my gaze drops to her mouth. Her pink tongue darts out to touch her bottom lip. When I meet her eyes once more, her pupils flare, and without thinking about what the fuck I'm doing, I lean in.

I don't have to go far because she meets me halfway, and our lips fuse, the attraction that has been steadily brewing under the surface between us for weeks boiling over. Taking one hand off the couch, I wrap it around the back of her neck and hold her to me, unwilling to give her a chance to get away as I lick the seam of her lips, gaining access. She tastes like cherries and feels like heaven.

My cock hardens behind my zipper, and the whimpering sound she makes in the back of her throat lets me know she's just as lost as I am. When her nails dig into my biceps, I pull her against me, then take her down over the arm of the couch, pressing my knee between hers and forcing her legs open. I settle over her, and she arches her chest into mine, then lets her head fall back, giving me access to the soft skin of her neck and upper chest.

I trail my mouth over the top of one breast as I cup the perfect handful. My cock throbs as she wraps her leg around the back of my thigh, and I'm just about to tear her shirt down to take her nipple into my mouth…when the doorbell goes off.

"You've got to be kidding me," I bite out, looking down the stairs at the front door, which I can see from where we are.

"Oh, my God," she whispers, and my eyes fly to hers. I know in an instant that not only is she freaked, but she's also going to bolt the second I take my weight away.

"Bridgett."

"I'm so sorry." She tries to scoot back on the couch.

"Babe."

"I don't know what happened."

"Look at me, Bridgett."

"I just—"

"Babe." I grab her jaw, not hard but enough to get her attention. "Look where you are."

"What?" She blinks, and I place my face over hers.

"You're under me."

"I—"

"I've wanted to kiss you since you told me the difference between expensive chocolate chips and the cheap shit you get at the grocery store."

"You have?"

"Fuck, yeah."

"Oh." She swallows, then jerks when the doorbell goes off again.

I swear to God, I'm going to kill whoever that is.

"Are we good?" I keep my eyes locked on hers, then wait for her to nod before moving and helping her up.

"I'm going to, um…" She smooths her hair, now in disarray, then starts down the stairs. "I'm going to put away the groceries."

"I'll get the door." I follow behind her, then catch her around the waist when she stumbles on the steps going down. "You okay?" I ask against her ear—not meaning to, but it happens. The way her body responds in a shiver says she likes it, which makes me want to do it again.

"Yeah." She clears her throat. "I'm okay." I let her go, then stay close until we reach the bottom landing. As soon as she's on solid ground, she rushes toward the kitchen while I head to the front of the house, adjusting myself.

Not that I need to do that. Because as soon as I look through the peephole and see my mother on the other side of the door, my dick deflates.

Fuck.

Chapter 13

Bridgett

Mom

Oh my God, oh my God, oh my God….
    I shakily go to the sink and turn the tap on cold so I can let the water run over my wrist to help cool me down. I can't believe I kissed Noah, or that he kissed me back. Not just that, I can't believe how flipping hot it was. I had no idea a person could be kissed like that. That you could practically orgasm from having a man's mouth on you and just his hand on your breast. I close my eyes and try to pull myself together, at least on the outside. Because Lord knows I'm a mess right now on the inside.

When I hear a woman's voice, my spine stiffens, then I hear Noah say, "Mom," and my stomach bottoms out. I glance around the kitchen frantically for somewhere to hide as footsteps get closer, but just as I start to step toward the pantry, Noah comes around the corner, his mother a few steps behind him.

"Babe." His gaze locks with mine, and I swear I see an apology in his eyes. "This is my mom, Rebecca. Mom, this is Bridgett."

"Nice to finally meet you." She steps toward me and startles me with a warm embrace.

"You too." I hug her back awkwardly. I don't know her, but I know *of* her. When Aiden was younger, he spent almost all his time at her house. I used to get so jealous of my brother because of his relationship with Noah and his family. They were always traveling for soccer—since he and Noah were on a team together—or going on trips to the lake or for weekends out of town. I wanted that. Wanted people who wanted me around. Because my mother made it very clear that I was an inconvenience, and my dad was always working. I was alone a lot, and that sucked. Okay, I wasn't alone all the time. I did have the people my parents *paid* to hang out with me, but that's not the same.

"I didn't mean to interrupt anything," she says, and I come out of my thoughts, finding her looking between Noah and me. "I was just in the area and thought I would stop by and see if you guys were home."

"You're not interrupting," I assure her quickly, feeling my face get hot. "Noah and I were just moving a couch upstairs."

His mom looks at him.

"I brought my bed over from the trailer and set it up for Bridgett in the spare room."

"Good." She gives him a nod of approval while my stomach flops all over the place. His gaze meets mine. I know he mentioned that he didn't want me sleeping on the couch, but I had no idea he was giving me an actual bed to sleep in.

"I also cleaned out the desk in there so you can use it, and I pulled a ton of hangers from my closet so you can hang up your shit."

"Thank you." I clear my throat because I do not want to start crying. Not in front of his mom.

Sheesh, how the heck am I supposed to convince myself not to fall for this guy when he's so sweet all the time?

I'm so screwed.

"Do you wanna hang out and stay for dinner? Bridgett's making lasagna." He picks up Lola when she walks out of the laundry room with her whining puppies trailing behind her.

"I don't want to intrude." She bends to pick up Coco.

"Mom." He shakes his head while I gather up Louie and Chanel, who swarm around my feet. And, no, I have not shared their names with Noah since I'm sure he would not approve or would make fun of me, especially when he calls Coco "Rocky," Louie "Ralph," and Chanel "Butch."

When silence descends over the room, I look up from kissing Louie and find Rebecca's eyes on me like she's waiting for me to tell her it's okay if she stays.

"I'm also making scones," I tell her stupidly. "But we're not eating those with the meal. I just found a recipe I want to try. With dinner, we're having asparagus and Italian bread." She smiles while Noah groans.

"Asparagus?"

"Asparagus is delicious, and it's good for you." I glare at him.

"It's gross."

"You've never had mine."

"True." He gives me a look that feels a little inappropriate with his mother standing just feet away.

"I'll stay," Rebecca says, and when I take my eyes off her son, I swear I catch her trying not to laugh. "I've never made scones before. Do you mind if I help?"

"I would love that." I set both puppies down and wash my hands. "I've only made scones once before, and they didn't turn out that great. But the new recipe I found seems easy enough for me not to mess up."

"Don't let her fool you, Mom. She's an awesome cook."

"I figured that much when you stopped coming by for leftovers."

I look at Noah as he shrugs, and my heart does a little double-beat. I knew that whenever I left food in the fridge for him, it ended up gone, but I didn't know how much he enjoyed it until right now.

"Do you girls want me to open a bottle of wine?" he asks, and I look at his mom, who shrugs as her eyes meet mine.

"Sure," I tell him. He goes to the pantry, coming out a minute later with a bottle of one of my favorite reds.

"I'll be right back," Rebecca says before heading toward the bathroom. I use that moment to grab my phone and pull up the recipe I found online.

As warmth hits my back, my hips sink into the counter in front of me, and I turn my head to the side to meet Noah's gaze.

"Are you okay?" he asks while grasping the curve of my waist in his large hand. My breath catches, and a tingle slides down my spine from the very intimate position.

Conner was not a big guy by any stretch. He always used swimming as a way to stay in shape, which kept him fit but thin. And at just a couple of inches taller than me, I never felt physically small in his presence. With Noah, it's the complete opposite. I feel tiny when I'm around him, even in my heels, and there is something almost euphoric about that.

"I'm good," I whisper, glancing toward the bathroom. Honestly, I'm shockingly relaxed, considering what happened earlier—even with his mom here.

"Okay." He gives my waist a squeeze and steps back, making me instantly miss his warmth.

"All right, I'm ready. Tell me what you want me to do." Rebecca comes around the corner, rolling up the sleeves of her sweater. I smile at her, then pass her my cell so she can look over the recipe.

"I've already frozen the butter," I tell her, going to the freezer to get it out.

"Oh, my," she whispers, and I look at her over my shoulder, finding her staring at my cell with a horrified look on her face.

"What?" I ask, walking toward her. Before I even make it across the kitchen, Noah is there, taking my phone from her grasp.

"I didn't mean to tap it," Rebecca says quietly as she looks at me, then up at him.

"What is it?" I try to see what he's looking at, but he hits the button on the side, turning the screen black.

"You don't need to see that shit." Noah grabs his keys before tossing my cell onto the counter.

"Honey." His mom reaches for him as I scramble to get my phone.

"Keep her here," he orders as I turn on my cell and try to find what they saw. Rebecca follows after him.

It only takes a second to locate the last message I got and see that it was from Conner. When I tap on it, I can only stare in disbelief at the text and image he sent me. In the middle of what used to be Conner's and my backyard is a pile of name-brand bags, shoeboxes, clothes, and even my jewelry box, with a red can of gasoline front and center. The message under it just reads: *I bet you talk to me now.*

"You've got to be kidding me," I mutter under my breath, then come out of my daze when I hear the back door slam shut. "Oh, no." With my heart pounding, I run down the hall and swing open the door, then stumble down the stairs as Noah backs his truck out of the garage.

His mom looks at me, wringing her hands, looking at a loss for what to do. "I couldn't stop him."

"Noah!" I scream while running to the front of his truck, slapping my hands on the hood.

"Bridgett." His mom rushes to me, grabbing my arm. "Let's go inside."

"I'm not letting him leave," I tell her, feeling panicked because I don't know what Conner might do if Noah shows up at the house. He's obviously lost it if he's going as far as burning my stuff to get my attention.

"Move, baby," Noah yells out the window, and I shake my head and circle around to the driver's side, where the glass is now rolled down.

"I don't care about any of that stuff."

"It's still your stuff."

"Yeah, but it's just stuff." I pull on the door handle to open it, but it's locked.

"Move out of the way, babe."

"Don't you understand that this is what he wants? He wants to get a rise out of me. He wants to upset me." I pull on the door handle again with no luck. "He doesn't get anything else from me. He doesn't get anything from you."

"Move," he instructs, and my eyes fly up to his.

"Please, don't do this," I beg, hating Conner more than I ever have, and that's saying something since I already despised him.

"Step back, baby," Noah orders quietly, and I do, even though I feel completely defeated. Dropping my gaze to the ground, I feel his mom's arms wrap around me. A second later, she lets me go, and before I have a chance to question why, Noah's huge body is wrapped around mine, and he's embracing me.

"Thank you." I sag against him, overwhelmed that he listened.

"I still want to kick his ass."

"He's not worth it." I tip my head back when his fingers go under my chin, putting pressure there.

"He's not worth it, but you are. You get that, right?" he asks, and tears fill my eyes. "Don't cry."

"I won't." I press my face into his chest so I can suck in a deep breath. The truth is that his words hit a part of me I didn't even know was vulnerable. For so long, I've felt like I'm not worth much of anything. That I'm a burden my family has just dealt with because that's what they're supposed to do. It's horrible to feel like nothing more than an obligation to people.

"Go inside with Mom," Noah says after a long minute, and every muscle in my body gets tight. "I'm not going after him." His lips rest against the crown of my head. "I'm just going to pull my truck back into the garage."

"Come on." Rebecca slides her arm through mine. I let Noah go with a nod and head into the house with her but stop right at the back door. "He'd never lie to you."

"I—"

Her quiet laughter cuts me off, and she takes my hand, dragging me down the hall. "He's always been brutally honest. I'm sure you'll find that out eventually because him being truthful doesn't always feel great." She grins. "That said, if he says he'll do something, he'll do it, and vice-versa." Her expression turns serious as she studies me. "Are you okay?"

"My ex is a jerk." I take a seat at the counter and watch her pour two cups of the wine Noah opened.

"I've been there, done that, sweet girl. And you're one hundred percent right about feeding into him. Guys like him get high off making other people miserable." She passes me one of the cups. "Noah's daddy was just like that, a liar and a master manipulator. That's why my boy is truthful to a fault and overprotective of the people he cares about." Her gaze on me goes soft, and my pulse quickens.

I lift my cup to my mouth, taking a sip of my drink as an excuse to get out from under that look. The red I always keep stocked isn't as good as the champagne I had last night, but that's probably a good thing since champagne tends to go to my head.

When I hear the back door open, my muscles instantly relax. Noah is back inside. As soon as he reaches the end of the hall at the entrance to the kitchen, his eyes meet mine before they scan my face.

"I'm gonna head up and finish with the couch. Are you two good?" He glances from me to his mom.

"We're good." She smiles, and with a jerk of his chin, he heads through the kitchen. A second later, I hear his boots hit the stairs. "Are you still up for making your scones?" Rebecca asks me.

"Yes." I get off my stool and wash my hands again, then Rebecca and I make blueberry-lemon scones that rival anything I've ever purchased from any bakery I've been to. Later that night, long after Rebecca has left and I'm in my new bed alone, I lie in the dark, not thinking about my ex. Instead, I think about the kiss Noah and I shared and how much I enjoyed every single second I've spent with him.

Which means I fall asleep happy and content, which is something new for me.

Chapter 14

Bridgett

Stuff

With a cup of coffee in hand, I look up from my computer when the back door opens, then frown when a multitude of voices travel down the hall, along with the sound of shuffling and banging. Curious about what's going on since Noah came downstairs about twenty minutes ago and went straight outside, I get off my stool and start to head toward the voices.

I don't make it more than a few steps because a man I don't know, carrying a stack of familiar-looking shoeboxes, blocks the hall to the garage door.

"Do you know where these go?" he asks, and I start to open my mouth but snap it shut when Noah comes up behind him, holding an armful of clothes that, again, look familiar.

"Just drop everything in the living room, John."

"Um…what's going on?" I ask Noah while another man follows *him*, his arms lined wrist-to-shoulder with different bags that I know for sure are the ones I left behind when I moved out of the house I shared with Conner. And I know this because when I was in London a couple of years ago, I purchased two Louis Vuitton bags at Hayes and had them both hand-painted with a pretty floral design by an artist in the store.

"The guys got your shit." Noah drops what's in his hands over the back of the couch, then turns to face me. "Or most of it."

"What?" I look from him to the pile on the couch.

"Your ex had already started to light your stuff on fire by the time we showed up," John explains before patting Noah on the back. "I'm gonna get the rest from the car."

"Thanks." Noah lifts his chin, and John heads down the hall, the other guy following him.

"I'm so confused." I shake my head, trying to wrap my brain around what's going on.

"I told you I wasn't going to confront your ex yesterday. I didn't tell you I wouldn't send someone else to do it." He shrugs.

"So you got my stuff?"

"Technically, John and Ed did."

"I…I can't… I don't know what to say." I watch John and Ed walk back in, carrying more of my things that they each dump onto the couch.

"You don't need to say anything," Ed cuts in, and I look at him. "We were told we'd get cookies as payback."

"Cookies?" I repeat, trying to keep up, which is difficult when I feel like this is some kind of odd dream.

"I told them you'd make them cookies," Noah says, and I nod. Because what else am I supposed to do?

"What are those?" Ed asks, and I turn to see him pointing at the scones sitting on a wooden cake plate under a glass dome. It's something I purchased at one of those stores that has everything from name-brand clothes to cookware at discount prices. Seeing it on the counter now, I bite my lip because although it looks good where it is, it's fancy and totally screams *a woman lives here, and this is her domain.* Not, *this is just something a bachelor uses to store cookies or baked goods in so he doesn't have to go searching for them in the pantry.*

"Scones, and you can't have any," Noah tells him, and I snap out of my runaway thoughts.

"Don't say that!" I gasp, turning his way.

"Baby, there are only three left. If they each take one, there's only one left for me."

"I can make more."

"You gonna make more today?"

"I wasn't planning on it." Then again, I had no idea he would eat half the dozen his mom and I made yesterday.

"Then they can't have any. They can get the cookies I told them you'd make."

"You can't be serious." I cross my arms over my chest and glare at him, which causes his friends to laugh.

"Don't worry. We won't take your food," John says and then looks at me. "We're gonna take off. It was nice meeting you."

"You too. And thank you for getting all this stuff."

"Can I get peanut butter chocolate chip cookies?" Ed asks before John can respond.

"Of cour—"

"You'll get what she makes you," Noah cuts me off.

"I'll make both of you whatever kind of cookies you want." I jab Noah in the side with my elbow, something that hurts me more than it does him.

"Thanks." Ed gives me a crooked smile.

"I'll take snickerdoodles," John requests, and a small laugh escapes from between my lips when Noah glowers at the two men, even as they head down the hall.

When I hear the back door open and shut, I look at the couch and coffee table in the living room, where my things have been piled high. There was a time when having name-brand things made me feel like I was somehow important. Like I belonged. Now, all I see is the money I spent so carelessly in my attempt to find some semblance of happiness and gifts my husband gave me to make me—or maybe himself—feel better about the fact that he couldn't keep his dick in his pants.

I didn't lie when I told Noah that all this stuff is just stuff and that I don't care about it. Really, I kind of wish his friends had left it to burn. Because now that it's all here, so are the memories that come with it.

"What are you thinking?" Noah asks, and I shake myself out of my thoughts and focus on him.

"That I want to start a fire in the backyard and toss all this in."

"What?"

I motion at the couch, then walk over and pick up a pink quilted vintage Chanel bag by its gold braided handle. "This purse cost almost eight grand." I watch his shoulders jerk back in surprise. "It was a gift from Conner after the first time he cheated on me—or at least the first time I found out." I toss it down, then pick up a slouchy black leather Gucci shoulder bag. "I bought this when I was in Paris. Conner was supposed to go with me, but he canceled on me at the last minute." I meet his gaze. "It was our honeymoon." I wave a hand out toward the couch. "Everything here has a sad, depressing memory like that."

"Babe," he says quietly, sounding as if he's in pain. I know I shouldn't like that my hurt bothers him, but I do because it shows he genuinely cares.

"Even though I really wouldn't mind burning it all, I know that would be stupid." I look at the stack of shoeboxes that all together probably add up to ten grand.

"Sell it all," he says softly while taking a step toward me. "Pay off your car and put the rest in the bank."

"Is that what you would do?"

"Yes." His hand curls around my waist, causing my stomach muscles to clench as his gaze locks on mine. "I know you said you don't want anything from that asshole, but he fucking owes you."

"I—"

He interrupts my protest by dropping a kiss to the edge of my mouth. It causes the breath I was about to release to get trapped in my lungs. "I'll move it all to the guest room upstairs until you're ready to deal with it." He lets me go, grabs an armful of stuff, and heads for the stairs.

"Thank you," I call to his back. He stops on the bottom step, then turns to look at me. "For this." I motion at the couch, then around the room. "For everything."

He opens his mouth like he's about to say something but then seems to think better of it. He shakes his head and continues up the steps without another word.

I stand there for a long moment, wondering what he was about to say, but I don't even have a chance to ask him because when he comes back down, he's dressed in a pair of jeans and a flannel button-down shirt with a vest over it. His cell is to his ear, and the second he hangs up, he lets me know that he has to head into work and doesn't know what time he'll be back. I know by the look on his face that I don't need to ask if everything is okay because it's obviously not.

Chapter 15

Noah

Home

Unlocking the back door, I let myself into the house with my duffle bag over my shoulder. I carefully nudge Lola back with the side of my sneaker so I can close the door in time to shut off the alarm. It's much later than I expected to be home, but there was a shooting involving two officers in town, so it was all hands on deck to find the person responsible. It took us hours, but before I left, we had a suspect in custody and word that both officers would be okay.

Once I punch in the code to reset the alarm, I kick off my sneakers, then bend to rub the top of Lola's head, giving her whining pups the same attention. After a couple of minutes, I head down the hall, noticing a light flickering in the living room. My gut twists when I hit the kitchen and spot Bridgett on the couch, asleep under her blanket, the TV on a local channel playing on low as a news anchor covers the shooting.

Fuck.

I should have thought to call her or send a message, but I didn't want to worry her. Dropping my duffle on one of the stools at the island, I walk into the living room and grab the remote off the table.

"You're home." Her sleepy voice sounds through the dim room before I can shut off the TV, and I watch as she sits, pushing her hair back away from her pretty face.

"You should be in bed."

"I was worried." Her gaze wanders over me, taking me in from my hoodie to my sweats. "You changed?"

"Showered at the station." I take off my sweatshirt, toss it onto the back of the couch, and sit next to her. She eyes me for a moment, then lunges and wraps her arms around me, burrowing her face against my neck. "I should have called."

"You were working," she whispers, and I close my eyes while dragging her onto my lap so I can hold her easier, not sure if it's her or me who needs the closeness more. "Did you catch the guys?"

"We did." I rest my lips against the side of her head. "They were hiding at a friend's house. It took some time to track them down, but when you've got every officer from here to Knoxville looking for you, there aren't many places you can lay low."

"And the officers?"

"Both of them should be released in a couple of days."

"Good." She pulls her head back, then rests her hand against my cheek and smooths her thumb over my bottom lip. "You scare me." Her gaze moves from my mouth to my eyes. "I've never worried about anyone but myself until you." She lets her forehead drop to my chin.

"Baby."

"I know that sounds horrible, but it's true. The idea of something—" She cuts herself off and shakes her head. "I can't handle that."

"Nothing is going to happen to me."

"You don't know that. You have one of the most dangerous jobs in the world."

"I now have a reason to make sure I make it home," I tell her softly. Her head flies up so her gaze can search mine.

"You—"

"You've turned my life upside down in just a few short weeks," I insert, then capture her face in my palms. "I wasn't expecting this. Or you." I shake my head. "I've tried telling myself that I need to keep my distance."

"You should."

"It's too late." I laugh. "Look at where you are right now, babe, and tell me that this shit doesn't feel right." I give her a minute to lie to me, to tell me that she doesn't feel like she fits in my arms, in my home, in my life. But she doesn't. She can't deny it, just like I can't.

Sliding my hand back into her hair, I drag her forward and brush my lips against hers. The cute little sound she makes in the back of her throat when I start to pull away and her fingers digging into my shoulders let me know she's not ready to end the kiss.

My cock, already hard from her closeness, becomes painful. I give her what she wants, using my hold to slant her head to the side and cover her lips with mine. I slide my tongue into her mouth and tangle it with hers, groaning as she straddles my lap, causing the heat of her through the thin shorts she wears to rub against my erection.

As the softness of her tits presses into my chest and her taste explodes on my tongue, I devour her, not sure I'll ever get enough or that I'll be able to stop.

"Noah," she moans, her hands going to my head as she lets hers fall back. Cupping her breasts in my hands over her thin tank, I nip my way down her neck, then groan as she rocks against me.

Flipping her onto her back, I settle between her spread thighs and wait until her lashes flutter open before placing my face close to hers. "We need to stop."

"What? No." She grabs my shoulders and wraps her legs around my hips. "Please, no."

"I'm trying to do the right thing."

"Me too." She leans up and nips my chin with her teeth. And just like that, whatever chivalry I had is gone. I cover her mouth with mine once more, reaching my hand between us to cup her sex. Even through the cotton of her shorts, I can feel how wet she is, and if I wasn't already on edge, that shit would send me over.

Sliding the material to the side, I slip my fingers between the lips of her smooth sex, and her hips buck as I easily find her clit and circle it.

"You're so fucking wet." I slip one finger inside her, then another, and bite back a curse. "And so tight. I'm gonna need to stretch my pussy out so I don't hurt it too bad the first time I fuck it."

"Oh my God." She pants, lifting her hips into my hand, her core clenching around my fingers as I lick down her neck to the tops of her breasts. "Noah."

"I know, baby. I feel it." I bite her nipple through the cotton of her shirt and use my thumb to roll over her clit. "I want all that wet heat wrapped around my cock."

"Yes," she breathes, leaning up so she can pant against my mouth. "I want that."

"You want me to fill you up?" I work my fingers inside her, loving the sounds she's unconsciously making and how good she feels around me.

"I…" Her head falls back. "Oh, goodness." Her legs, still wrapped around me, tighten as her pussy begins to flutter. Watching her start to fall apart has to be one of the most beautiful things I've seen in my life, and it obviously takes her by surprise because she almost looks panicked. Before she can overthink it, I cover her mouth with mine, and she instantly relaxes, her body taking it from there, climaxing before she goes limp.

I slowly ease my fingers out of her and smile at the contented expression on her face. "You okay?"

"No." Her lashes flutter, and she nibbles her bottom lip. "I…" Her cheeks darken. "Never mind."

"What?"

"Nothing." She looks away as she attempts to sit up. Something impossible to do with me still holding her hostage with my weight between her legs.

"Talk to me."

"I've never had an orgasm." She covers her face with her hands, and my muscles bunch.

"Pardon?" I lean back and pull her hands away so I can look at her.

"You heard me."

"I did, but you can't be serious."

"Why would I lie about that?" She laughs without humor while shoving at my chest in an attempt to get me to move.

"Never? With anyone you've been with?"

"I've only been with one person." She shoves at me harder. "I thought something was wrong with me."

Fuck, it should not make me feel smug that the dick she was with couldn't even get her off, but it does. That said, I know guys like him, and he probably made her feel like it was her fault when that's the furthest thing from the truth.

"There is nothing wrong with you." I grab her wrists and hold them against me while placing my face close to hers. "He didn't know what the fuck he was doing."

"He said—"

"There it is," I growl, starting to get pissed. "I bet he said a lot of shit, baby, and we've established that your ex is an asshole." I pull her up and over until she's straddling my lap again, then grab her hips and hold her tight so she can't get loose. "Fuck him, everything he said, and every lie he told you to make himself feel better." I squeeze her hips. "You came easy for me."

Her pupils dilate.

"I did?" She clears her throat, then whispers, "Is that a bad thing?"

"Do you feel how hard I am?" I lift my hips into hers, and her breath catches. "Getting you off turns me on. Knowing I can make you lose it so easily…" I shake my head. "I could become addicted to that, to making you lose it."

"Oh." She rests her hands on my chest, and I can tell from the look in her eyes and how her chest starts to rise and fall a little more quickly that she likes knowing that.

Taking my hand from her hip, I smooth it up her back and capture the back of her neck so I can use it to drag her mouth down to mine. The kiss starts slow, but it heats up fast. Her soft hand moves down my chest to under the top of my sweats, and my dick throbs as her fingers brush against the head. "Shit."

"Is this okay?"

"Your hand on my dick is definitely okay," I clip out, and she grins against my mouth as she wraps her fingers around my cock and pulls it out of my sweatpants before dragging her hand up and down the length.

"You're so hard and so soft," she whimpers.

"You keep fucking with me, baby, and I'm going to come in your hand."

"Would that be a bad thing?"

"Since I want to come inside you, yes," I growl, and her breath catches while her hand around my dick jerks.

"Do you have a condom?" she asks. I still because I don't have one. It's been months since I've been with anyone, and like an idiot, I thought that if I didn't have any when she moved in, I could avoid this exact moment.

"No." My jaw locks, and her eyes meet mine.

"I'm on birth control." She holds her breath as she waits for me to respond, and I soften my tone as her hand stills.

"I love that you want to give that to me, baby, but we gotta be safe. I know you said your ex stepped out on you."

"I haven't been with him in ages and had a check-up since to get tested for everything." Her hand stills. "Sorry, I don't want to pressure you."

"Pressure me?" I laugh. "You're not pressuring me. You're tormenting me." I push the light material covering her sex aside. "I want to fuck you. I also want to do right by you."

"Okay," she agrees, and I move my eyes to the space between us, to her hand wrapped around my dick while my thumb moves over her clit, then down to her tight opening.

"We should stop."

"We should." She rocks her hips as I move my other hand to her ass and lift until she's holding my cock in line with her pussy.

"I've always done the right thing." I take my hand off her ass and wrap it around her waist.

"I know." She begins to sink down my length, and my dick throbs. Gritting my teeth, I bite back the urge to come, which is difficult to do with how hot and wet she is while wrapped around me.

"Oh…" Her eyes, dark with desire and locked on mine, widen as she finally takes all of me.

"You're gonna have to get used to my size, baby." I rock my hips back, then up into hers, before sliding my hand forward and using my thumb to roll over her clit.

"Noah." Her forehead drops to mine as her pussy starts to flutter. "That can't be normal."

"It's normal." I circle her clit and rock into her, listening to her breathing quicken while her nails dig into my shoulders. Knowing I'm about to lose it because she feels too fucking good, and I've wanted this for so fucking long, I speed up my thrusts while working her clit.

It works. She tightens around me, so much so that it's almost unbearable, and I plant myself deep inside her, holding her there as I come. And as cheesy as it sounds, the moment feels like I'm finally home.

Chapter 16

Bridgett

Lay It Out

With my heels clicking on the tile floor, I head down the hall toward Edgar's office with the file he requested in hand. It's Monday, and although I usually dread coming to work after the weekend, there is a pep in my step and a smile on my face that I can't shake.

To say I'm happy is an understatement, and my good mood has everything to do with going to bed with Noah last night and waking up in his arms this morning. Not that I had much choice about sleeping with him since he carried me up to his bed, where he stripped us of our clothes, then held me until I fell asleep.

It didn't take long. Between the relief of him being safe and home and two orgasms, I passed out almost the minute my head hit the pillow. Waking up was a lot more difficult, but having him get up and shower with me definitely made for a great start to the day.

As I get closer to Edgar's office, my footsteps slow because I hear a multitude of voices, my name and my brother's, and some not-so-nice language. Anger curls in my stomach as I listen to the men who have worked for my father for years talking about us like we're nothing more than pests they have been forced to deal with. And although it hurts to hear them badmouth about me, it pisses me off that they're talking about my brother.

Aiden made it clear for years that he never wanted to work for my father, but when our dad had his stroke, he agreed to come home and fill our dad's shoes—something that wasn't easy for him to do. Our dad wasn't the kind of boss to leave all the work to the people under him. No, he ran everything himself, only delegating certain projects to the people he hired.

For weeks after his stroke, no one seemed to know up from down, and if it weren't for Aiden, I have no doubt the business would have gone under.

With a much-needed deep breath, I walk the rest of the way down the hall to Edgar's office and step inside without waiting for him and the other men in the room to acknowledge me. Five sets of eyes turn my way, but I keep my gaze locked on Edgar's as I toss the file in my hand onto his desk.

"Here's the file you asked for." I glance around the room, catching the eye of each man standing there. Men I know my father has trusted for years. Men looking at me like they have been caught with their hands in the cookie jar.

"I know I just started working for Bender and Sons and that I have a lot to learn about the company and my place here, but I think each of you needs to be reminded that this is Aiden's and my father's company.

"Bridgett—" Edgar starts, but I hold up my hand.

"I do not care how you feel about either of us. I do not care if you think we deserve the positions we have. I *do* care about you talking about us like we don't matter. Because we do." I glance at everyone again. "This is our dad's company, and if I ever hear you talking negatively about Aiden or me again, I will go to our father. And if you know anything about him, you know he's always wanted to keep Bender and Sons a family business, which means it won't be Aiden or me without a job. It will be you."

With that final statement, I turn on my heel and head out of the office and down the hall to my desk, feeling like a weight has been lifted off my shoulders. I don't know how my dad would feel about me doing what I just did, but I feel fricking fabulous, like I should be offered an Academy Award.

When I hit my desk, I grab my purse from my drawer and dig through it for my cell phone so I can send Noah a message to let him know what just happened. I might not know how my dad or Aiden will react to what just happened, but I do know Noah will be proud of me for standing up for myself.

Just as I finish sending him a text, I hear footsteps approaching. When I look up, I spot Catharine coming my way. I haven't seen her since

I was out with May weeks ago. As soon as our eyes meet, I can tell something is off. She might be dressed in a pretty, expensive jacket, jeans, and boots with her hair fixed and makeup done, but she looks pale and nervous.

"Hey," she whispers when she's close. I place my cell on my desk so I can message Noah once I figure out what's going on with her.

"Hey," I parrot, then ask, "Are you meeting someone?" I mean, people purchasing property or a home don't usually come to this location, but what the hell do I know?

"No." She licks her lips. "I came to talk to you." She glances around the empty office space. "Do you have a couple of minutes to talk?"

"Sure." I look at the conference room. When my dad was here, everyone in the office had weekly meetings in there, but it's been empty since. "Come on." I lead the way, letting her inside before me and then shutting the door. After we both take a seat at the large oval table, I watch her, wondering what this is all about.

"I don't even know how to say what I'm going to say," she says quietly, ducking her head, then I listen to her take a deep breath. "Conner and I are having a baby."

My spine stiffens—not in anger or shock, but in a what-the-heck-are-you-doing-here-and-why-the-hell-are-you-telling-me-this kind of way.

"I need you to sign the divorce papers he gave you."

"What?" A laugh escapes, and she lifts her head to glare at me.

"I know he gave you divorce papers. I need you to sign them so he and I can get married." She rests her hand on her stomach, probably to remind me that she's carrying his child.

"I don't know what Conner told you, Catharine, but I've already signed the divorce papers."

"Don't lie." Her nostrils flare. "He told me you've refused to sign them until he gives you the money you asked for."

"Is that what he said?" I try really hard not to start laughing, but it's honestly difficult, given the situation.

"He told me everything." She sits up a little straighter in the chair she's in, no longer looking as unsure or ill as she did earlier. "I know you cheated on him and that, even when he forgave you for forsaking your vows, you didn't stop sleeping around. And now you're trying to get every single penny you can from him."

"I think you and Conner need to have an honest conversation about what's really going on," I tell her gently because getting upset cannot be good for her or the baby if she is pregnant.

"He's always honest with me," she snaps while slapping her hand down on the top of the conference table, making me jump. "For once, think about him and how what you've done has affected him."

Taking a breath, I think about trying to tell her again that I already signed the divorce papers, and that *Conner* is the one refusing to jot his name on the dotted line, but I can tell by her demeanor she won't believe me. "All right." I stand. "I'll sign the papers."

"What?" She blinks up at me.

"I'll sign the papers."

"You will?"

"Absolutely." I shrug and head toward the door, ready for this awkward conversation to be over. I hear her get up.

"How will I know you're being honest about signing the papers?" she asks, stepping out of the conference room as I hold open the door.

"If he doesn't have them from my lawyer by tomorrow, you can stop by, and I'll give you a copy," I tell her, and it hurts me to see her so relieved by my response. I know her trust in Conner is misplaced, but I can see she has to learn that difficult lesson all on her own.

"Thank you."

"Mm-hmm." I watch her walk toward the hall that leads to the exit, and as she disappears out of sight, I hope like heck Conner does right by her and the child she's carrying.

* * * *

Sitting on the front porch, I watch Lola, Louie, Chanel, and Coco wander around in the thick grass of the front yard. When I got home from work this evening, I decided to bring the pups outside to explore—something they hadn't been big enough to do until now. I wasn't sure they would take to the change of environment, but from the minute we got outside, they started exploring every blade of grass and haven't stopped since.

When I hear a car coming down the driveway, my stomach instantly starts to flutter. Noah sent me a text letting me know he would be home in time for dinner, which is a bonus with his new position. I guess the overnight shifts he had been working are a thing of the past. Or maybe they'll just be few and far between now.

As a familiar car comes into sight through the trees, the flutters in my stomach instantly turn to anxiety.

"Lola," I call, and her head flies around before she starts running my way. Thankfully, all the puppies follow her lead. "Come on, guys. Hurry."

I pat my thigh and open the door to the house as Conner parks his car at the edge of the walkway.

"Bridgett!" he shouts as I try to get the puppies inside.

"Go away, Conner!" I yell back without looking at him, my attention on the pups circling my feet and Lola, who is now barking. Just when I start to step inside, hoping the dogs will follow, he snatches my biceps in a tight grip. "Let me go."

On instinct, I spin toward him and shove his chest with all my might. Instead of releasing me, he stumbles off the step, taking me with him. I hit the ground hard, my hip taking most of the impact while he lands on his back with a grunt.

He groans. "We need to talk."

"No." I scramble to my feet and try to make it to the door, but his hand goes around my ankle, tripping me. I fall face-first toward the concrete steps, barely catching myself with my hands while my knee slams into the edge of the stair. A surge of adrenaline and anger flood my system, and I flip around to my bottom and start kicking, not caring one single bit where I hit him.

"Stop it! I just want to talk to you." He yelps when I catch him in the jaw with the edge of my foot, but he doesn't release me. Instead, he grabs the foot that just kicked him and stands.

"Let me go!" I scream, but he doesn't. Instead, he yanks me fully down the stairs, causing my head to hit the ground with a thud.

"Shut the fuck up!" he roars at Lola, then tries to kick her. Thankfully she's nimble and quick, and he misses.

Seeing red, I sit, grab hold of his hands, and dig my nails into his skin. That does it. He lets one of my feet go, and I use the opportunity to kick him again. This time, I make direct contact with his crotch, and he releases me and falls to his knees, grabbing his junk.

"You kicked me in the balls!" he howls as I quickly get to my feet.

"You deserved it, you dick. You tried to kick my dog!" I step toward him with plans to kick him again but scream when arms wrap around me, and I'm lifted off the ground.

"It's just me," Noah says in my ear. My body goes limp against him. He drops me to my feet, then spins me around to face him and grasps my face. "Are you okay?"

"I think so," I pant, only realizing then just how out of breath I am and how hard my heart is pounding.

"All right." He touches his lips to my forehead, then says, "Go inside, call 911, then grab my duffle from the laundry room and bring it out to me."

"Okay," I agree, and he lets me go. I run toward the house, and as soon as I'm up the steps, I hear a scuffle and Conner shouting. I turn to find Noah shoving him face-down in the yard and placing my ex's hands behind his back. Knowing Noah probably wants his handcuffs from the duffle, I run to the laundry room first, then grab my cell phone on my way back through the kitchen, dialing 911 as I head outside.

"You can't arrest me!" Conner screams, fighting Noah to get loose, which is about as pointless as an ant fighting a lion.

I carry the bag across the yard to Noah while telling the dispatcher on the phone what happened and that we need an officer to come out. Before I disconnect, she tells me she has someone en route and less than ten minutes away.

"They're on the way." I watch Noah pull Conner off the ground once the cuffs are on.

"Good job, baby."

"So you two are together now, huh?" Conner asks as Noah walks him toward the driveway.

"Shut up, you idiot," I snap at him. "Seriously, I don't even know why the hell you showed up here. You should be home with your pregnant girlfriend."

"He's having a baby with someone?" Noah asks me.

"Yes. She came into my office today, asking me to sign the divorce papers I've already signed." I roll my eyes, and he grunts.

"I came to tell you that you and I can be together. That we can raise the baby."

"Oh my God, you really are an idiot." I laugh. "And your plan to get me back involved manhandling me and dragging me around?"

"You put your hands on her?" Noah asks, sounding so scary a chill slides down my spine.

"That wasn't supposed to happen," Conner says quickly, then adds, "She shoved me."

"You grabbed me!" I yell at him, then watch in awe as Noah picks Conner up, his feet a good twelve inches off the ground, before slamming him down to sit on the tailgate of his truck with enough force the truck bounces.

"I'm going to take your badge for abuse!" Conner yells at him.

"You try to do any such thing, I'll press charges," I yell at him, and he snaps his mouth shut. "Sign the divorce papers, Conner, and leave me the hell alone, or I swear to God I will press charges and then tell anyone who will listen about what you did."

"Babe, you're pressing charges anyway," Noah says, and I tip my head back to meet his gaze.

"What?" Conner asks, looking panicked.

"He showed up here and put his hands on you. You're pressing charges, and he's going to jail," he continues without even acknowledging Conner, who's started to wiggle and is trying to get down off the truck.

"I'll sign the papers," Conner says. I look at him. "I'll do whatever you want. I can't go to jail. My parents would kill me."

"You're going to jail, motherfucker."

"Do you swear you'll sign the papers?" I ask, hearing Noah growl.

"Yes, I'll sign them right now. They're in my car."

"Is it unlocked?" I ask.

"Yes." He nods frantically. "They're on the back seat," he says. I walk to his car parked in front of Noah's truck and open the back door. When I see the papers along with a pen, I pick both of them up.

"Bridgett." Noah steps in front of me, and I rest a hand against his abs.

"This is the one thing I want."

"Fuck." He groans, then glares at me. "At some point, I'm gonna get good at telling your ass no and sticking to that."

"Okay," I whisper, trying not to smile so I don't make him angry. Taking the papers and pen from me, he walks them over to Conner, then pulls a key out of the pocket of the coat he has on.

"It looks like today is your lucky day," he grumbles to Conner, dropping the papers onto the tailgate of the truck before uncuffing him. "Sign them," Noah bites out, and Conner hops down, flips open the folder, and starts to sign. I let out a relieved breath when he finishes, then take the papers from him and hold them against my chest.

"Now, listen to me for once and go inside, babe," Noah says. I don't push my luck. Instead, I head across the yard, and just as I hit the front porch, two police cruisers pull up.

I stand just inside and watch three officers and Noah gather around Conner, and I can tell by the panicked movements Conner's making they are scaring the crap out of him. I probably shouldn't be happy to know he's so intimidated, but given what happened just a little bit ago, I am. A few minutes pass before they let him get into his car, then Noah and the guys talk a bit before they shake hands, and the officers get into their cruisers.

As Conner and the officers turn around in the yard so they can head down the driveway, Noah gets in his truck and drives it toward the garage. I close the front door and walk through the house to meet him.

The second he steps inside the back door, I run toward him. He doesn't hesitate to wrap his arms around me and pick me up. "He signed the papers." I smile down at him.

"He did." He carries me down the hall toward the kitchen. "I still wish he was going to jail."

"Sorry." I rest my hands on his chest as he plants my ass on the counter, placing himself between my thighs.

"I'll find a way for you to make it up to me."

"That might sound like a threat, but I have a feeling it's not." I smile, and he chuckles while cupping my face between his palms.

"You know, now that you're divorced, I'm keeping you."

"Are you?"

"Fuck, yes." He kisses me, and I kiss him right back.

If someone had told me months ago that I would be living with a man and falling in love, I would have laughed and laughed.

But I guess things have a funny way of working out for the best, even when you think you're at your lowest.

Epilogue

Bridgett

Two months later

"May and Aiden are here, baby," Noah says, coming into the kitchen behind me and kissing the side of my neck.

"Did you turn on the grill?"

"I did." He gives my waist a squeeze and then lets me go when the doorbell rings. "I'll get it."

"Okay." I accept a quick kiss, then watch him walk around the corner and out of sight before I go back to putting the finishing touches on the cake for dessert.

Since Conner signed the divorce papers two months ago, life has been a whirlwind of many ups, with a few downs tossed in.

A week after my lawyer pushed the divorce papers through, a judge signed them, finalizing my divorce and ending that chapter of my life.

Then, a couple of days after, Noah took my brother out for a beer and told him that the two of us were together. I was honestly torn about him telling Aiden; not because I worried that Aiden wouldn't like his best friend being with his little sister, but because I was worried Aiden wouldn't want *me* with *Noah*.

I fretted the entire time Noah was out that evening, scared that he would come home and say that he'd changed his mind about me after talking to Aiden.

I shouldn't have worried.

Aiden had concerns, most of them having to do with how quickly things had progressed between Noah and me. But he told Noah that if he was happy, then he was happy *for* him. And I know deep in my gut that even if Aiden had told Noah that he didn't think it was smart for him to be with me, my guy wouldn't have listened.

Noah has made it clear that his feelings for me are genuine and that he's in this for the long haul. He's accepted me as I am and is patient with me as I figure out who I'm becoming.

"It smells delicious in here," May says by way of greeting, coming around the corner into the kitchen, carrying a bottle of wine in one hand and a bouquet in the other. Aiden and Noah follow behind her.

"It's Noah's twice-baked potatoes." I give her a one-arm hug, then smile at my brother as he walks around the counter to kiss my cheek.

"No, it's the cake. The frosting on that thing is killer," Noah tells them with his gaze locked on mine. I feel heat rising to my cheeks at the memory of what he said he wanted to do with the frosting he swiped from the bowl earlier.

"Don't gross me out before we eat," Aiden grumbles, looking between the two of us. May giggles while I duck my head.

"So…" May bumps her hip into mine, and I look at her. "How's the new job?"

"Good. Busy." I shake my head. "There's lots to learn, but I really love it."

"She's already outselling Manny, and he's been at that location for three years. Everyone is seriously impressed with how well she's done in such a short time," Noah tells her, and the pride I hear in his voice makes my chest warm.

Honestly, it feels good knowing that people are taking notice of how hard I'm working. And I'm doing it all on my own. I mean, yes, I have someone showing me the ropes, but I could have gotten this job even without my dad's help.

"So, what's your plan now that your dad's back in the office?" Noah asks Aiden, and I hold my breath because I know that working for our dad has always been a sticky subject for him. But it's a good question, especially since my dad started coming to work daily last week.

He's improved tremendously in the last couple of months and is almost back to one hundred percent. He also seems happier now than he ever has. I don't know if that has to do with divorcing my mom or what, but it's been good seeing him as he has been.

On the other hand, my mom is still as angry as ever. But I haven't spoken to her since our last run-in, which had to do with me being with

Noah—whom she doesn't think is worth my time. When she told me to dump him, I told her that she wasn't welcome to be a part of my life in any capacity unless she made some significant personality changes. And since I doubt she'll change, I'm not sure I will ever see her again. And that makes me sad for her because, at the end of the day, she will be missing out on being a part of her grandchildren's lives one day. My dad, however, is thrilled that I'm with Noah, which only makes me feel surer about the man I've fallen in love with.

"I'm staying." My brother's statement brings me out of my thoughts, and I find him looking at May, who now sports a huge rock on her ring finger. "Dad's back, but he doesn't want to work the hours he was before. So, I'll fill in for him when he needs time off and still deal with clients like I have been."

"Glad to hear that, man," Noah says, and May leans into my brother while I lean into Noah.

Looking at everyone in the room, I feel a sense of peace wash over me. Not only do I have a healthy and strong relationship, but I've also got the family I always wanted.

And I doubt anything is better than that.

* * * *

Noah
Four Months Later

Walking into the house, I lock the door behind me, then head down the hall toward the kitchen, not surprised that Lola and Chanel do not come to greet me. When Bridgett is home, they stick to her like glue.

Not that I blame them since I tend to do the same myself.

Bridgett isn't in the kitchen or living room, so I step into the spare I converted back to an office for us to use after moving Bridgett's shit to my room the weekend after we got together. Finding it empty, I go upstairs because I know she's home since her car is in the garage. I hit the bedroom and do a scan, finding the bathroom door closed with a light shining out from under it. Hearing what sounds like crying, my heart stops, and I walk over to the door and shove it open. I don't know what I expect to find inside, but it's not Bridgett sitting on the floor, surrounded by a half dozen plastic sticks.

"What's going on?" I bark, and her tear-filled eyes widen as they lock on mine.

"You're home." She frantically reaches for the sticks, and it suddenly hits me like a ton of bricks what they are.

"You're pregnant." I step into the room and drop to my knees in front of her, grabbing one of the tests before she can hide it. Looking at it, I see two lines, but I have no idea what that means.

"I…I didn't know. I swear I haven't missed any of my pills. I—"

"Are you pregnant?" I cut her off, and she nods while her chin wobbles.

"I'm sorry." She covers her face with her hands, and my gut twists.

"Baby." I wrap my arms around her and pull her against my chest. "Please, don't cry."

"I swear I'm not trying to trap you." She sobs, and I laugh because she trapped me long before this moment. "It's not funny, Noah."

"Baby, I've been trying to figure out how to trap you since you moved in." I fall to my ass so I can curl her onto my lap, then whisper, "So, we're having a baby?"

"Yes." She sniffs.

"I guess we should get married then."

"What?" She jerks her head back to look at me.

"I figured I'd ask you in a few months anyway, so we can just do that now."

"You're not upset about this?"

"Are you?" I ask. Because, really, I feel surprisingly okay with her carrying my child, even if we might be doing things backward. Then again, we've been doing everything backward since the beginning. I mean, fuck, she was still technically married when we got together—not that I have any regrets.

"Yes." She rests her hand on her still-flat stomach. "I…I'm scared, but I'm also happy."

"Me too, baby." I rest my forehead against hers and cover her hand with mine. "I love you so fucking much."

"I love you too," she whispers, kissing me quickly before resting her forehead in the crook of my neck. As I sit there on the bathroom floor with her in my lap, all I can think about is how crazy life is sometimes. Because I had no idea she would come into my life and give me everything I didn't know I wanted.

Sign up for the 1001 Dark Nights Newsletter
and be entered to win a Tiffany Key necklace.

There's a contest every month!

Go to www.1001DarkNights.com to subscribe.

As a bonus, all subscribers can download FIVE FREE exclusive books!

Discover 1001 Dark Nights Collection Ten

DRAGON LOVER by Donna Grant
A Dragon Kings Novella

KEEPING YOU by Aurora Rose Reynolds
An Until Him/Her Novella

HAPPILY EVER NEVER by Carrie Ann Ryan
A Montgomery Ink Legacy Novella

DESTINED FOR ME by Corinne Michaels
A Come Back for Me/Say You'll Stay Crossover

MADAM ALANA by Audrey Carlan
A Marriage Auction Novella

DIRTY FILTHY BILLIONAIRE by Laurelin Paige
A Dirty Universe Novella

HIDE AND SEEK by Laura Kaye
A Blasphemy Novella

TANGLED WITH YOU by J. Kenner
A Stark Security Novella

TEMPTED by Lexi Blake
A Masters and Mercenaries Novella

THE DANDELION DIARY by Devney Perry
A Maysen Jar Novella

CHERRY LANE by Kristen Proby
A Huckleberry Bay Novella

THE GRAVE ROBBER by Darynda Jones
A Charley Davidson Novella

CRY OF THE BANSHEE by Heather Graham
A Krewe of Hunters Novella

DARKEST NEED by Rachel Van Dyken
A Dark Ones Novella

CHRISTMAS IN CAPE MAY by Jennifer Probst
A Sunshine Sisters Novella

A VAMPIRE'S MATE by Rebecca Zanetti
A Dark Protectors/Rebels Novella

WHERE IT BEGINS by Helena Hunting
A Pucked Novella

Also from Blue Box Press

THE MARRIAGE AUCTION by Audrey Carlan
Season One, Volume One
Season One, Volume Two
Season One, Volume Three
Season One, Volume Four

THE JEWELER OF STOLEN DREAMS by M.J. Rose

SAPPHIRE STORM by Christopher Rice writing as C. Travis Rice
A Sapphire Cove Novel

ATLAS: THE STORY OF PA SALT by Lucinda Riley and Harry
Whittaker

LOVE ON THE BYLINE by Xio Axelrod
A Plays and Players Novel

A SOUL OF ASH AND BLOOD by Jennifer L. Armentrout
A Blood and Ash Novel

FIGHTING THE PULL by Kristen Ashley
A River Rain Novel

VISIONS OF FLESH AND BLOOD by Jennifer L. Armentrout and
Rayvn Salvador
A Blood and Ash/Flesh and Fire Compendium

A FIRE IN THE FLESH by Jennifer L. Armentrout
A Flesh and Fire Novel

Until May

Until Him/Her 11
By Aurora Rose Reynolds

When May Mayson signed up with a popular dating app, she never thought she would get catfished. After being stood up for a date, she finds out that the man she'd been talking to for weeks was lying about who he is.

After that horrible experience, she changes her number and deletes the app… only to have fate shove Aiden Bender right into her path.

The famous ex-soccer player whose photo was used to bait her on the dating app is the last person she expects to come face-to-face with in real life. Now, suddenly, he's everywhere she is.

With his soccer career over after an injury, Aiden is sure his shot at happiness is lost. Then he meets May, a woman he can't seem to get enough of. Now, all he has to do is convince her he's not playing a game—while juggling his father's construction company, blocking the flow of women his mother keeps sending his way, and avoiding getting run over, and shot at by whoever is out to get him.

There's a game being played, and neither May nor Aiden understand the rules.

* * * *

I take a drag from my beer, then almost choke when I see the girls hit the deck of their house and a gorgeous brunette stands up to talk to them. The short, white, almost-sheer sundress she's wearing blows in the wind around her, making her look angelic.

No fucking way.

I blink, sure that I am imagining things, but when she looks in our direction and our eyes lock, I know I'm not.

May.

Jesus, what are the odds she'd be here?

I stopped by her house twice since I saw her last, but she didn't answer either time. I wasn't sure if she was home and avoiding me, or if she was out, but I promised myself that when I got back, I would track her down. *Looks like I don't need to do that*, I think as I watch pink infuse her cheeks before she drags her eyes off mine.

"You good?" Carlo asks, nudging my shoulder, and I pull my

attention off the house as the three women disappear inside.

"I know the brunette," I mutter while turning toward him.

"You know May?" Troy asks, and my hand tightens around my beer at the familiar way he says her name.

"A few days ago, I was pulling into one of the housing developments my dad just started building on, and she was there, dragging a kid out of a pond that had iced over."

"Christ," he mutters, looking toward the beach house.

"She saved the kid's life."

"She's a nice girl." His eyes lock with mine, and for the first time since meeting him, I want to punch him in the face. He's interested in her; it's obvious. Normally, I would shrug that shit off and let him take his shot.

But not with her.

No fucking way.

About Aurora Rose Reynolds

Aurora Rose Reynolds is a *New York Times*, *USA Today* and *Wall Street Journal* bestselling author whose wildly popular series include Until, Until Him, Until Her, Underground King, Shooting Stars, Fluke My Life and How to Catch an Alpha series.

Her writing career started in an attempt to get the outrageously alpha men who resided in her head to leave her alone and has blossomed into an opportunity to share her stories with readers all over the world.

Discover 1001 Dark Nights

ABANDON by Rachel Van Dyken ~ THE OPEN DOOR by Laurelin Paige ~ CLOSER by Kylie Scott ~ SOMETHING JUST LIKE THIS by Jennifer Probst ~ BLOOD NIGHT by Heather Graham ~ TWIST OF FATE by Jill Shalvis ~ MORE THAN PLEASURE YOU by Shayla Black ~ WONDER WITH ME by Kristen Proby ~ THE DARKEST ASSASSIN by Gena Showalter

COLLECTION SEVEN
THE BISHOP by Skye Warren ~ TAKEN WITH YOU by Carrie Ann Ryan ~ DRAGON LOST by Donna Grant ~ SEXY LOVE by Carly Phillips ~ PROVOKE by Rachel Van Dyken ~ RAFE by Sawyer Bennett ~ THE NAUGHTY PRINCESS by Claire Contreras ~ THE GRAVEYARD SHIFT by Darynda Jones ~ CHARMED by Lexi Blake ~ SACRIFICE OF DARKNESS by Alexandra Ivy ~ THE QUEEN by Jen Armentrout ~ BEGIN AGAIN by Jennifer Probst ~ VIXEN by Rebecca Zanetti ~ SLASH by Laurelin Paige ~ THE DEAD HEAT OF SUMMER by Heather Graham ~ WILD FIRE by Kristen Ashley ~ MORE THAN PROTECT YOU by Shayla Black ~ LOVE SONG by Kylie Scott ~ CHERISH ME by J. Kenner ~ SHINE WITH ME by Kristen Proby

COLLECTION EIGHT
DRAGON REVEALED by Donna Grant ~ CAPTURED IN INK by Carrie Ann Ryan ~ SECURING JANE by Susan Stoker ~ WILD WIND by Kristen Ashley ~ DARE TO TEASE by Carly Phillips ~ VAMPIRE by Rebecca Zanetti ~ MAFIA KING by Rachel Van Dyken ~ THE GRAVEDIGGER'S SON by Darynda Jones ~ FINALE by Skye Warren ~ MEMORIES OF YOU by J. Kenner ~ SLAYED BY DARKNESS by Alexandra Ivy ~ TREASURED by Lexi Blake ~ THE DAREDEVIL by Dylan Allen ~ BOND OF DESTINY by Larissa Ione ~ MORE THAN POSSESS YOU by Shayla Black ~ HAUNTED HOUSE by Heather Graham ~ MAN FOR ME by Laurelin Paige ~ THE RHYTHM METHOD by Kylie Scott ~ JONAH BENNETT by Tijan ~ CHANGE WITH ME by Kristen Proby ~ THE DARKEST DESTINY by Gena Showalter

COLLECTION NINE
DRAGON UNBOUND by Donna Grant ~ NOTHING BUT INK by Carrie Ann Ryan ~ THE MASTERMIND by Dylan Allen ~ JUST ONE

WISH by Carly Phillips ~ BEHIND CLOSED DOORS by Skye Warren ~ GOSSAMER IN THE DARKNESS by Kristen Ashley ~ THE CLOSE-UP by Kennedy Ryan ~ DELIGHTED by Lexi Blake ~ THE GRAVESIDE BAR AND GRILL by Darynda Jones ~ THE ANTI-FAN AND THE IDOL by Rachel Van Dyken ~ CHARMED BY YOU by J. Kenner ~ DESCEND TO DARKNESS by Heather Graham~ BOND OF PASSION by Larissa Ione ~ JUST WHAT I NEEDED by Kylie Scott

Discover Blue Box Press
TAME ME by J. Kenner ~ TEMPT ME by J. Kenner ~ DAMIEN by J. Kenner ~ TEASE ME by J. Kenner ~ REAPER by Larissa Ione ~ THE SURRENDER GATE by Christopher Rice ~ SERVICING THE TARGET by Cherise Sinclair ~ THE LAKE OF LEARNING by Steve Berry and M.J. Rose ~ THE MUSEUM OF MYSTERIES by Steve Berry and M.J. Rose ~ TEASE ME by J. Kenner ~ FROM BLOOD AND ASH by Jennifer L. Armentrout ~ QUEEN MOVE by Kennedy Ryan ~ THE HOUSE OF LONG AGO by Steve Berry and M.J. Rose ~ THE BUTTERFLY ROOM by Lucinda Riley ~ A KINGDOM OF FLESH AND FIRE by Jennifer L. Armentrout ~ THE LAST TIARA by M.J. Rose ~ THE CROWN OF GILDED BONES by Jennifer L. Armentrout ~ THE MISSING SISTER by Lucinda Riley ~ THE END OF FOREVER by Steve Berry and M.J. Rose ~ THE STEAL by C. W. Gortner and M.J. Rose ~ CHASING SERENITY by Kristen Ashley ~ A SHADOW IN THE EMBER by Jennifer L. Armentrout ~ THE BAIT by C.W. Gortner and M.J. Rose ~ THE FASHION ORPHANS by Randy Susan Meyers and M.J. Rose ~ TAKING THE LEAP by Kristen Ashley ~ SAPPHIRE SUNSET by Christopher Rice writing C. Travis Rice ~ THE WAR OF TWO QUEENS by Jennifer L. Armentrout ~ THE MURDERS AT FLEAT HOUSE by Lucinda Riley ~ THE HEIST by C.W. Gortner and M.J. Rose ~ SAPPHIRE SPRING by Christopher Rice writing as C. Travis Rice ~ MAKING THE MATCH by Kristen Ashley ~ A LIGHT IN THE FLAME by Jennifer L.

On Behalf of 1001 Dark Nights,

Liz Berry, M.J. Rose, and Jillian Stein would like to thank ~

Steve Berry
Doug Scofield
Benjamin Stein
Kim Guidroz
Tanaka Kangara
Asha Hossain
Chris Graham
Chelle Olson
Kasi Alexander
Jessica Saunders
Stacey Tardif
Dylan Stockton
Kate Boggs
Richard Blake
and Simon Lipskar

Made in the USA
Columbia, SC
15 February 2023

12408493R00071